"Eat," Jake Ordered, Glaring At Her.

Morganna hesitated. She tried to remember the proper etiquette for roast campfire rabbit—fingers or fork? She eliminated the idea of using a salad or dinner fork, simply because none was offered.

A scream split the misty night air. Morganna jumped; Jake just sat sipping his coffee. "Cat. A big one," he told her.

"A cat? Out here?" Morganna asked, wondering how such a small household animal could survive on this mountain.

"Cougar. Wolves and coyote, too. This canyon is a favorite grazing ground of elk and moose. They've been circling all day, waiting for us to leave."

"You mean they've been out here the whole time?" Morganna's voice was high-pitched, squeezing through her tight throat.

"Those are bear marks on that tree at the edge of the clearing. Big cat marks aren't far from here. They're marking their territory against intruders."

Morganna just gulped.

Dear Reader,

This month we have a very special treat in store for you. It's the Silhouette Desire "Premiere" author for 1993! This is a completely new, never-before-published writer, who we have chosen as someone exciting and outstanding. Her name is Carol Devine, and her book is *Beauty and the Beastmaster.* There is a letter in it from her to all of you, her new fans. *Who* is the Beauty and just who—or what—is the Beastmaster? Well, I'm not telling; you'll have to read and find out.

In addition to our "Premiere" author, October has five more favorites. Our *Man of the Month* is from the delightful Cait London. The lineup is completed with wonderful books by Jackie Merritt, Christine Rimmer, Noelle Berry McCue and Shawna Delacorte.

As for *next* month...it's a winner! We've decided to "Heat Up Your Winter" with six of our most sensuous, most spectacular authors: Ann Major, Dixie Browning, Barbara Boswell, Robin Elliott, Mary Lynn Baxter and Lass Small. Silhouette Desire...you just can't get *any* better than this.

All the best,

Lucia Macro
Senior Editor

CAIT LONDON
THE SEDUCTION OF JAKE TALLMAN

SILHOUETTE *Desire*®

TM Published by Silhouette Books New York

America's Publisher of Contemporary Romance

SILHOUETTE BOOKS
300 East 42nd St., New York, N.Y. 10017

THE SEDUCTION OF JAKE TALLMAN

Copyright © 1993 by Lois Kleinsasser

ISBN: 0-373-05811-X

First Silhouette Books printing October 1993

All the characters in this book have no existence outside the imagination of the author and have no relation whatsoever to anyone bearing the same name or names. They are not even distantly inspired by any individual known or unknown to the author, and all incidents are pure invention.

Printed in the U.S.A.

Books by Cait London

Silhouette Desire

The Loving Season #502
Angel vs. MacLean #593
The Pendragon Virus #611
The Daddy Candidate #641
Midnight Rider #726
The Cowboy #763
Maybe No, Maybe Yes #782
The Seduction of Jake Tallman #811

CAIT LONDON

lives in the Missouri Ozarks but grew up in Washington and still loves craggy mountains and the Pacific Coast. She's a history buff and an avid reader who knows her way around computers. She grew up painting landscapes and wildlife, but is now committed to writing and enjoying her three creative daughters. Cait has big plans for her future—learning to fish, taking short trips for research and meeting people. She also writes as Cait Logan and won the *Romantic Times* Best New Romance Writer award for 1986.

To my readers who enjoyed *Midnight Rider* and
wanted to read more of the Blaylock men.

One

———

"**I**s my daughter a dragon lady?" Nathaniel Larrimore repeated Jake's question too cautiously. The telephone lines stretching from the Larrimore Corporate Headquarters in Kansas City, Missouri, to Jake Tallman's ranch home crackled slightly with the late-April storm hanging over Colorado. "You're quick, Jake. I said Morganna was a corporate woman, unused to relaxation and camping in the wilds. I said she isn't used to fending or cooking for herself. That's why this whole idea of a 'women's bonding expedition' is crazy."

Jake eased his dusty work boots up to his scarred desk, carefully placing them away from the legal pad filled with notations about his dream—a vocational training school. Morganna Larrimore had probably had every advantage when she was growing up, her world far from rural Colorado, where money and miles often decided a child's education opportunities.

Orphaned at ten by a drunk who held up a convenience store, Jake had fought the love of the Blaylocks when he'd been claimed at fourteen. In the four years between his parents' deaths and the Blaylocks collecting him, he'd learned basic, ugly facts that continued to scar other young lives. While Morganna had been choosing party dresses for high school proms and college sorority dances, the young people in his rural community were working to survive, dismissing education as a luxury.

He glanced outside to the sheets of rain pelting his living room window. With unseasonably warm temperatures, a spring thaw was melting the deep snow quickly, and heavy rains added to the freakish weather, creating serious flooding and mud slides.

"We go back a long way, Nathaniel," Jake said quietly. "You were there when Dianne and our baby died. I'll get your daughter down safely." A familiar heavy ache settled around his heart. Ten years ago Nathaniel Larrimore had been on a hunting trip, roughing the wilderness when he found Dianne's battered car down that embankment. Endangering his life to fight the raging river torrents, Nathaniel had extracted Dianne, pregnant with Jake's son, from the wrecked car. In a makeshift shelter, Nathaniel had made Dianne comfortable in her last moments. Jake fought the dull shaft of pain. Jake's son would have been ten now, the ranch house would be filled with excitement and Dianne would be—

Jake pressed his lips together, forcing back the pain. Swerving a vehicle to avoid hitting a mule deer and her fawn was a common occurrence in mountainous country and had cost Dianne her life and Jake's future. At forty-one, he'd never met anyone who could fill his heart like Dianne, and it wasn't fair to give a woman less than everything that marriage entailed.

"A dragon lady." Nathaniel mulled over the idea before continuing. "Some employees might call her that. She's stubborn and has a temper to match mine. Since I'm asking you to risk your life, I might as well level with you, Jake. Morganna is a dyed-in-the-wool, high-powered female executive. A real tornado. She'll end up marrying a whining little SOB who jumps when she barks. At thirty-five, Morganna is a tough-nosed little snob, and I made her that way. She is *not* soft and charming. Good Lord, Jake, I'll wager she'd manage to unhinge anyone with a pittance of your patience."

Jake sipped his coffee. Business flowed through Larrimore's blood, not the warmth of family ties. However, Jake suspected that Nathaniel deeply loved each of his four wives in different ways. He cared for both his children, but all the Larrimores had a precarious, warlike relationship. Nathaniel worried that Paul, his son, would never be able to hold his own, while he warily respected his daughter's abilities and strength. Of a traditional nature, Nathaniel wanted Morganna balancing his grandchild on her hip, not a corporate ledger. As the weaker Larrimore personality, Paul was balanced between Nathaniel and Morganna.

Through the years, whenever Jake had guided Nathaniel in the high mountains, the male respect and friendship had deepened. On vacation, the businessman had a devout respect for the land and the animal life that inhabited it.

Jake narrowed his eyes, seeking the Rocky Mountain Range through the layers of heavy rain and low-hanging clouds. The mountain Nathaniel's daughter had picked for a "women's bonding expedition" was dangerous. Filled with spongy ground, raging streams and mud and snow avalanches, Big Thorn challenged an experienced woodsman. Rugged rocky buttes led to beautiful alpine meadows and higher mountain peaks that never lost their caps of snow. A hunter's paradise, the area was filled with cougar, bear and mountain sheep. Deer returned to the high mountains in the summer, lounging in the shade of the pines and fir. But now in April, Big Thorn Mountain defied vehicles; passage on foot or with a horse was life threatening.

"Ah...there's couple more things, Jake," Nathaniel continued. "The first one is that I'd rather you kept quiet about my request. Morganna gets furious when she knows I'm pulling strings...."

He hesitated, then took a deep breath. "She may not be ready to come off that mountain. The helicopter returned for them and the other four women—her staff—left against Morganna's wishes. She refused to leave...called them mutineers and weaklings. I understand she bullied them into the primitive camp, the female-bonding fiasco, in the first place. She's used to getting her way. The company gossip is that every one of those four women swear they will never work for or come close to my daughter again."

Jake inhaled slowly. If Morganna's personality was as near Nathaniel's as he suspected— "You mean I may have to pry her off Big Thorn?"

"Take my advice. A smart man doesn't force Morganna to do anything. He challenges her. Just one more thing, Jake. I'm going to ask that you keep Morganna under wraps for a month or so. There's a maniac making threats on her life. We're on his tail and hope to grab him before Morganna returns to the office. We haven't got all the details yet."

Jake shoved his notes for the vo-tech school into the desk's drawer. With Nathaniel's list growing by the minute, Jake would be busy for weeks. "Anything else?"

"Just one little thing. She's a crack shot. Taught her myself," Larrimore said proudly.

After replacing the receiver, Jake settled down to enjoy his last cup of coffee in a warm, dry room. He stared into the flames crackling in the living room's huge rock fireplace. He'd tracked lost persons before, depending on the Apache and Spanish hunting blood he shared with the massive Blaylock family. His great-great-grandfather, Moses Tallman, had once tracked and fought a killer bear up on Big Thorn and barely lived through the winter. With the Blaylocks, Jake's father had hunted and found several lost children and a few wayward campers. They'd retrieved a few persons from Big Thorn; one had perished in a hospital a week after rescue.

If the dragon lady was half as tough as her father thought, half as stubborn, she just might be alive.

He cradled a pottery mug of hot coffee in his hands, savoring the warmth. At seven o'clock he'd already completed the morning chores and had settled down to spend the rainy, chilly morning on accounting books that begrudged the slightest purchase for his three-hundred-acre ranch. Beads of pitch ignited in the fireplace, sending out a spray of sparks to light his home.

Renovating a pioneer log cabin had filled the long, lonely hours between dawn and dusk. The stark, scarred, primitive furniture that filled the house suited Jake. The muted shades of crockery bowls and pebbled, blue enamel plates blended on the shelves of rough lumber he'd built in the area that served as the kitchen. At the opposite end of the room, Jake had selected wide, contemporary windows that offered a view of the sprawling, scenic wilderness of pines and fir. An enormous couch with a solid wood frame and tan cushions was a concession to his loneliness, a place to lie and stare into the fire. A place to fight what might have been.

The shards of his life with Dianne lay in a pioneer trunk against the wall, and the means to fill his lonely nights rested in covered baskets along another wall. Beads and leather lay in one basket, cotton rags for braided rugs in another, and small chunks of wood for carving were neatly packed away. He liked his life neat, free from any emotional hardships— he'd had enough to last a lifetime.

Tossed carelessly aside, a soft woolen throw woven by Hannah Blaylock caught the glow of the firelight in shades of mauve, tan and pale blues.

His carving tools, carelessly placed in a long, wooden pioneer trencher, rested next to a hand-held tape recorder. Rambling across a thick, rough mantel were his small animal carvings, a flute and a glass kerosene lantern.

Children listened to his tapes, their fingers exploring his carvings. Without sight, these children cherished his stories of animals and the beauty of the land. A small company in New Mexico blended Jake's flute music and his stories, providing tapes to the children who would "see" with their ears and fingers. With Jake's help, a four-year old boy was already learning the flute, playing music from the beauty of his soul. People unaccustomed to Native American music could easily confuse it with "New Age."

To the northwest of his ranch lay another home, one filled with children and laughter, the small farm he had once shared with Dianne. Gleaming in the firelight was a hand-made walnut rocking cradle, the only furniture he had taken from that house.

Jake rubbed his chest, forcing his mind to the Larrimore woman and the danger waiting on Big Thorn.

Four hours later Petey Vasques spat a wad of tobacco into the mud and drew his yellow rain poncho closer. The small, wiry cowboy held the reins to Black Jack, Jake's big Appaloosa stallion. The powerful horse was edgy; stamping and rearing slightly as thunder sounded over the pounding, heavy rain. Petey huddled against the side of Jake's battered green pickup truck and muttered, "Boss, you got no daylight and nothing but mud slides, snow and floods ahead of you. What about sending that chopper in again?"

Jake worked quickly, securing the tarp over the camping gear on the pack mule, Pinky. He jerked the brim of his western hat down, blew away a stream of water that ran from the brim. "Cougar Rim Canyon is too narrow. Her camp is located on that meadow at the base. The sound of the chopper could cause an avalanche of snow or mud, maybe rocks that have been loosened by the thaw."

He checked the saddle cinch, his rifle, then nodded to Petey who said, "Hell of a day for a joy ride, boss. Mad Duck Creek is flooding, and Paco Pass was closed because of a mud slide. With luck you'll take a good two days reaching Cougar Rim, if the old bridge isn't washed out. If the weather turns bad, you could be in snow. Sure you don't want me to come along?"

"Stop mothering, Petey," Jake returned gently, certain that Petey's bones were too fragile for the trip. "Watch for Tyree Lang. If he turns up, see that he eats some vegetables, okay?"

"Talking about mothering, boss," Petey tossed back. "I'll watch out for the kid. There's tea bags in your pack...women like tea sometimes, if they're edgy. There's one of those small bars of scented soap from Mitch's Motel, too. I figured it was better than that heavy-duty stuff we use."

Jake nodded, levering up on Black Jack and settling himself in the saddle. Tyree Lang at sixteen reminded Jake of himself—uncertain, wary of a friendly hand. Like Jake, the boy had been orphaned at an early age and passed around foster homes. At sixteen, Tyree was walking the crossroads, too much time on his hands without attending school and going nowhere fast. He'd been on the wrong side of the law once or twice and Jake had stepped in to help. He wanted to do more, but Tyree was wary of attachments. Jake understood perfectly; it hurt like hell to have love jerked away on a whim of fate or man.

Thunder rumbled overhead, and his thoughts swung to the woman in danger and Big Thorn's mud and rock wilderness. Jutting apart from the Rocky Mountains like an elite god, Big Thorn was twice as dangerous as a wounded cougar. Jake nudged the horse toward the thick stand of pines hovering in the mist like guardians of Big Thorn. The narrow trail wound slowly away from the road, and through the sound of the rain, Jake heard the truck engine rev, the old horse trailer rattling as Petey drove away.

That night Jake camped in a meadow away from the raging white-water creek. He placed Black Jack and Pinky beneath a tarp strung from trees, then worked quickly, building a fire and settling in for the night. Savoring the dregs of coffee from the thermos in the small, dry tent, Jake ate Petey's sandwiches and listened to the wilderness night closing around him.

He lounged naked on his down-filled sleeping bag, the small camping lantern heating the tent and drying his damp boots. The custom-made sleeping bag was a luxury, a concession to his six-foot-three height. He pushed his fingers through thick, straight hair, a reflection of his Native

American heritage, and crossed his arms behind his head, settling in for the night. He enjoyed the crisp cold air, the dampness prowling over his skin, bonding him to his ancestry.

The men in the Tallman family clung to their heritage, lying in the wilderness, the cold mist settling on their naked bodies. For generations they had initiated their sons to the spiritual strength and essence of nature. To the colors of earth and sky, the beauty of shape and texture, of wind and freedom and the stories of animals. Jake allowed the colors to come inside him infrequently, to swirl and hover and cleanse him. Since the series of foster homes and the boys' school, he had forced back the sight of his inner eyes, the need of his hands to stroke color into pictures. That doorway would remain closed, set apart from him like the pain of those early, boyhood years.

He placed a hand over his heart, riding the slow heavy beat. As the last of his family, Jake had ached for a son to hold, a daughter to spoil, and fiercely wanted a woman to love.

With Dianne he'd had a taste of happiness, then a cruel breath of nature swept his life away. Instinctively he knew there would be no other woman to take as his mate, to cherish, to warm his heart and bed.

There were women fascinated by his dark, angular looks, who boldly sought him out. The Blaylock family periodically tossed prospective mates at him, but despite a few sparks, Jake had escaped easily. Celibacy wasn't easy after Dianne, but he couldn't share his body and not his heart, his spirit. He'd had a taste of heaven, of belonging, with Dianne and he wouldn't mar that sweet memory with a quick sexual farce that left him empty and cold.

Jake lay in the darkness and listened to the rain pelt the tent, willing away the shadowy ache.

The woman in Cougar Rim Canyon would be cold now. She'd be frightened, ready to come with him. After a week of camping with the women and another three days by herself, Morganna Larrimore would have had enough cold nights and rain to last her for a lifetime. According to Nathaniel, Morganna had chosen a primitive method of camping, taking few implements with her and relying on her manuals and dubious skills to provide food and shelter.

A branch fell in the forest, startling the animals. Black Jack whinnied and Pinky brayed furiously. Though both animals were suited to the hazardous trip, strong and surefooted, they wanted their dry hay and barn. They had crossed several flooding creeks during the day, taking their time to find safe footing on the rocks and melting snow, and then pushing up rock and mud embankments with every ounce of strength in their powerful muscles.

Jake frowned, reminded of the city woman stranded on top of Big Thorn. A relative of the extensive Blaylock family, Jake had been tracked down, straightened out with love and taught that women were to be respected and cherished. Morganna Larrimore would probably resent any indication of respect for her femininity, and taking it as a weakness, would toss it back in his face.

He shifted uneasily, aware of a rock bruise on his shoulder blade. He'd gotten the bruise from falling down a mudslicked bank. Whatever, whoever Morganna was, she'd have to be tough to safely return from Big Thorn, even with his help.

Morganna huddled beneath the thatch of limbs, perching on a sodden log and clutching her damp sleeping bag around her. She wouldn't cry, not even if the tears could be disguised in the penetrating, cold rain that had fallen for a week and two days. She sniffed, her lids burning with tears she refused to shed. "They're all cowards," she said, admitting at once that she had been talking to a raven sitting like a buzzard waiting for a dead body.

The huge bird sulked in the gray sheets of rain. He hunched beneath a dripping bush and waited for the remainder of the granola mix Morganna had been desperately hoarding. She dipped into the waxed paper sack and retrieved the last raisin—the one she had been saving for dessert after the last soggy nut, which had served as both lunch and dinner. Wild game was to have subsidized the primitive camping menu. She soon discovered that she didn't have the heart to ruin a poor fish's mouth with a hook or dig a pit and trap something cute and furry with pretty brown eyes. She tossed her head. "This was a good idea, really. I formatted and developed the whole method of co-worker bonding. My father aptly pointed out that I seem to have a problem communicating with women employees. That they resent my organized—and, might I add—very efficient business techniques. They totally resented my handbook—it was a stroke of genius. The dress code was absolutely necessary with the varying skirt lengths. The mandatory course on successful list making should have been appreciated."

She carefully placed the raisin in her mouth, sucking it. "Corporate bonding away from the day-to-day business environment is highly recommended. We had perfect how-to-survive manuals. The opportunity to refresh and relax while learning to work together for a mutual cause would have really benefited Larrimore Corporation. So many misunderstandings can arise from a simple lack of people skills. This was a perfect time to meditate and structure our lives, which is exactly why I insisted my personal staff accompany me... although I just couldn't convince Rita to invest in bonding. I really needed her to stay at the helm, anyway."

She sniffed again, glaring at the bird who impatiently stalked back and forth on the bough and returned her glare. "I just wanted to equate. To be recognized as their equal and develop some sort of rapport to show Dad that women can bond as easily as men. To show him that I can develop friendships and thus streamline my staff away from petty disagreements. I am *not* an unbalanced workaholic—a term my father uses frequently when he finds I've put in a few extra hours at the office. I can relax like any other woman. *I can.*" She realized belatedly that she had been screaming at the bird and her throat was quickly becoming raw.

A stream of cold water ran from the sleeping bag covering her head to her throat, startling her, and she swallowed the precious raisin. She shivered, drawing the bag closer and hoped the raisin would expand to fill her empty stomach. "The manuals will dry when it stops raining. Survival techniques should be reasonably easy. My father camps all the time, using very little. It's just a matter of reading the right material . . . which I will, once it's dry."

Leaning back against the rough bark of a pine tree, Morganna stared sullenly at the bird. "I have rations to last for a week . . . if I'm careful." She touched the crushed, last bag of granola in her breast pocket for reassurance; she had lost several foodstuffs to the churning creek, in which she had placed them to keep cool. "I'll start a fire—" She glanced at the sodden, black coals representing her foiled attempts at fire making and sniffed. "Actually, Mr. Bird, everything is going according to schedule. In the wilderness, you see, there are forces we can't control, therefore we must learn to survive under any conditions. . . ."

She truly hoped the trail of warm water dripping from her cheek wasn't a tear.

"I can survive without modern conveniences and without the taste of business blood. I will . . . I really will." She ached in every joint, her flesh chilled. A hot, bubbly bath with a cup of tea would be heaven now. Morganna pushed her chattering teeth together. She didn't have that tub, nor that steaming cup of tea. She did have the intelligence to overcome this rough patch. When the helicopter arrived to pluck her off the mountain in four days, she would have a beautiful, organized and functioning survival camp.

Then she sneezed.

The next afternoon Pinky balked at the bottom of a muddy hill, his long ears twitching. He stared at the hill while Jake stood at the top of the twelve-foot incline. Pinky planted his back legs apart and refused to move, despite Jake's threat to serve his ears to the buzzards and roast his carcass over a spit.

At the top of the incline Jake wrapped Pinky's rope around a tree trunk. He braced his feet apart, his hands on his hips beneath the rain slicker. The clouds had changed, the wind sending the mixture of rain and snow against his skin like tiny, sharp pellets. With luck he'd reach the woman before nightfall and before the snow. He ground his teeth, glaring at the placid mule who stared at that same spot on the muddy bank. "If you don't come up here, you pitiful excuse for a mule, I'm coming down."

Running low on his famed patience, he pivoted momentarily to trace a deer's zigzagging path through the woods. Then he jerked up his leather gloves, grabbed a bush and started down the bank. The bush's roots loosened from the soil, and Jake slid on his backside to lie at Pinky's front hooves.

The mule brayed once, nodded, then fought his way up the bank. His powerful back legs propelled him easily to the top, where he brayed loudly. Jake jerked to his feet, swiped his hat from his head and slapped it against his muddied jeans. "You buzzard bait."

Pinky peered over the edge of the incline at Jake. The mule watched with interest while Jake fought his way back to the top. He swung into Black Jack's saddle, tugged up the collar of his jacket beneath the slicker and refused to look at the mule.

Ms. Larrimore and his mule shared a stubborn trait, and it was enough to drive a sane man into madness. Whoever Morganna Larrimore thought she was, she would get a piece of his mind. There were certain basic truths in life. One of them was that a city woman didn't belong on top of a damned dangerous mountain, refusing to leave when good sense dictated she should. Jake's upper arm ached bitterly, a reminder of his fiery years when he thought showing off for a female was honorable, proof of his manhood.

Jake heard his teeth grind as Black Jack snorted, white steam rising in clouds from his flaring nostrils. In the deep stand of pines a limb weighted with rain crashed to the ground. Jake inhaled slowly. He wasn't a half-baked youth now. But he was angry, very angry. Unused to the emotion, it settled on him like a cloak of burrs.

He reached Morganna's camp at nightfall, when the layers of gray mist blended with the few fat flakes of snow. The higher elevations of Big Thorn loomed above him in a smoky blue gloom.

Morganna's camp—or what was left of it, spread across a good section of the alpine meadow. A hatchet lay in the mud next to a log that had been dragged across a sprawling puddle. Rope tangled in the top of a young serviceberry tree, and wads of paper floated in a wide mud puddle. Clothing lay, crumpled and sodden, on bushes, and a raven strutted over to a clutter of empty cans and papers, picking at them with interest. For a moment Jake scanned the deserted camp and fought the cold fingers of terror. The woman could be anywhere on the face of the mountain. She could be lying in the ravine he had just passed—

"You are trespassing," a feminine voice stated firmly from the shadowy depths of a haphazard lodge of branches. "I've got a gun and can use it quite skillfully. State your reason for being here."

The voice was husky, low and very feminine. Jake nudged Black Jack with his boots, urging him closer to the shelter. A pistol shot whizzed over his head, Black Jack reared and Pinky strained at the lead rope. For the next few seconds Jake worked fiercely to settle the animals. With the rock face of Big Thorn ready to come down, all he needed was a stubborn woman with a loaded gun. "Don't shoot," he said quietly and waited for a second shot that didn't come as the seconds stretched by.

"Obviously that was a warning shot, or I would have hit you. Why are you here?"

Jake swung down from the saddle, walking slowly toward the hovel of branches, his hands away from his body. Above him a rock bounced down the face of a rugged cliff and his heart stopped as he waited for an avalanche that nothing could stop or outrun. After a moment's silence he crouched in front and leaned to look inside. From the darkness of a sleeping bag, she said firmly, "If my father sent you, you can go. I'm perfectly fine. Everything is under control."

Morganna evidently had a burr under her saddle where her father was concerned. Jake decided that for the moment it was better to avoid telling her the true reason why he was cold, wet and angry.

The pistol shot reminded him that he was dealing with a woman bearing Larrimore's tough, no-nonsense genes. A dragon lady. "Just passing through, ma'am," he said easily, and wondered how far he could pitch that fancy little pistol. "I'm heading on home to my ranch."

Jake fought for a view of the woman seated on the log and shrouded by the wet sleeping bag. The bag's outer cover was waterproofed and very expensive. However Morganna's bag's external cover was on the inside and the soft inner lining was exposed to the rain dripping through the gaping branches.

He saw the muzzle of an automatic pistol, then two small boots, which slid back under the bag. A pale, fragile hand grasped the sleeping bag to close it. Clearly Morganna wouldn't be swayed by her father's concern, judging by the defensiveness in her voice. "Don't shoot me, ma'am. I'm looking for a place to set up camp. This looks better than the rest."

Water dripped steadily from the brim of his hat, and a snowflake fell between them. He glanced at the low clouds, the mist swirling around him. "May snow tonight. Are you warm enough in there?"

"I'm fine...quite comfortable. You may set up your camp some distance away from mine and spend the night. Just don't interfere with my quiet and relaxation," she said, then sniffed.

"You need a fire, ma'am," Jake said quietly, trying to find her face in the shadows. His boot crushed a sodden, empty sack of granola, making a soft, swishing sound. "You can share mine if you like."

She jerked the muzzle of her gun, indicating he leave. "I'm just fine. I'll make my own fire in a few moments.... Right now I'm bonding with nature. A little dry tinder under the branches and a match and I'll have a fire, too. Please leave."

Straightening slowly, Jake dipped his hat because he had been taught always to tip his hat to a lady. There were times when a man didn't argue, and this was one of them. He glanced at the sodden black coals and the wet firewood—green wood, hacked straight from a live tree. If Morganna wanted warmth and food, other than the trail mix of nuts and granola, she would have to come to him. He glanced at the empty bags crumpled in a puddle and the open, empty knapsack hanging from a limb. He would wait her out, then take her down the mountain safely. He couldn't fight Pinky and a mulish woman at the same time.

In half an hour Jake's fire blazed, the aromatic smoke curling lazily upward to blend with the mist. In the shadowy distance he glimpsed a small woman dressed in a bulky camouflage jacket. She worked furiously over the dead camp fire then retreated into the hovel for a few minutes. She tried to start the fire again, dragging the ripped, sodden sleeping bag with her.

In another half hour he had braced a green branch over his fire and hung a coffeepot over it. Expertly erecting his camp, Jake pitched the tent and constructed a lean-to of branches to protect his fire and provide lounging space. In short order he cared for the animals, collected wood, then settled down to cook a huge steak and fried potatoes over his camp fire. He expected the woman to step from the gloomy mist at any minute. When she didn't, he called gently into the night, "I've got plenty for two. Steak and potatoes. Coffee, too."

There was just the slightest hesitation, then she returned loftily, "Please be quiet. You're frightening the animals and ruining my relaxation period."

"Females and mules," Jake muttered, turning the steak in the large skillet. He ate slowly, making certain that his movements were outlined in the fire for her benefit. From his first encounter, Jake decided that his quarry could not be forced, but might be tempted to act sensibly. While he sipped coffee, she attempted another furious fire-making session, then stalked back to her hovel. Jake scowled at that defiant little mess of branches. If she lasted another night without catching pneumonia, she'd be lucky. He'd have a hell of a time getting a sick dragon lady off the mountain, let alone a blue-blood city woman. The combination would be a disaster.

A snowflake landed in his coffee and melted instantly. Another flake swirled along his neck and Jake glanced into the night, unable to find the woman's camp in the darkness. At any minute she would decide that pride wouldn't fill her stomach or warm her body. She'd be reasonable by morning, and they could return to his ranch.

Nathaniel Larrimore's daughter needed a few lessons, and Jake was just the man to teach them to her, before her father collected her stubborn bones.

Three hours later Jake cursed, flipped back the sleeping bag cover and jerked on his clothes. Morganna couldn't learn those badly needed lessons if she was frozen to death. He jammed on his boots and stepped out into the two-inch snow. The branch hovel looked like a big snowbank as he walked toward it, warily expecting a bullet to whiz by his ear.

Jake eased in front of her hovel, crouching to look inside. Within the sodden sleeping bag she lay balled like a child. He caught a blur of a pale face and a small hand resting beside it. Morganna was deeply asleep and didn't protest as he removed the Italian-made pistol from her limp fingers. He snapped the clip out and carefully placed the gun in the weatherproof container nearby. When Jake eased Morganna from the sodden bag, she sighed deeply, placing her cold nose against the warmth of his throat.

Two

Morganna snuggled against the cove of heat surrounding her. A hard, warm length followed her back to her knees and down to her feet. She burrowed deeper, feeling small and protected and heavenly warm. Her head rested on a hard pillow, which was slightly uncomfortable. She smiled dreamily, reveling in the warmth that had replaced the unbelievable chill lodged deep in her bones. Her feet rested on a heating pad and she wriggled her bottom, edging closer to all that glorious, wonderful heat. The weight across her waist was pleasantly heavy and crisp with hair— Hair! Morganna opened her eyes to see a huge pair of worn, muddy boots standing six inches from her face.

Over her head a soft but discernable snore rhythmically fluttered a strand of her hair.

Her back was laminated to something hard and hairy. Then lower, pushing at her intimately was the unmistakable arousal of a man.

By the time her heart started pumping again, she was fighting desperately. Kicking with all her might, Morganna landed a hefty blow and was rewarded by an astonished, solid grunt. Raising her head sharply, she connected with his chin and his teeth clicked shut. "What the—"

She moved quickly, pummeling and kicking, using every ounce of her body as a weapon. The man cursed solidly, his large body confined by the zipped sleeping bag. She connected with that distinct male arousal, and he exhaled sharply, doubling over immediately. The action trapped her against the limits of the bag, just as his legs clamped around hers and his arms wrapped her tightly. "Lady, I suggest you calm down," a disgruntled male commanded between his teeth. She struggled, testing a strength that would not yield. Panting heavily, she realized suddenly that she was naked.

The man in the sleeping bag with her was naked.

She blinked. *They were both naked.*

Rummaging quickly through her limited knowledge of lovemaking, Morganna established that the man had not violated her.

He effectively cut short her next bid for freedom, tucking her head beneath his chin and overpowering her easily with his size. "What the hell is wrong with you?" he muttered in a dangerous tone that sent chills down her spine.

She panted heavily, aware of how easily he controlled her body, one hand securing both wrists. Each time she took a breath, her breasts pushed against his forearms, and there was no question about the thrusting male form behind her hips. Morganna closed her eyes, her heart racing. "You may release me. I'm ready to get up now," she said imperiously.

"You are?" he asked too quietly, after a moment's hesitation.

"Yes. Obviously you thought you were helping. My clothes were damp and you probably stripped them and shared your...your body warmth to help me. But I'm used to survival in the worst elements and there was really no need for all this effort."

His arms tightened gently, and she thought she felt him nuzzling her hair. "There wasn't?" She frowned, blowing a long black silky strand away from her face. His tone had changed to a low, sensuous invitation.

"Absolutely not. You can release me now, Mr. . . ."

"In view of the current situation, you can call me Jake. Jake Tallman."

"How do you do. Morganna Larrimore." She twisted slightly trying to turn, and her nose jammed against a hard, male shoulder. "If you'll just release me."

"You aren't going anywhere, Morganna." The deep voice tested her name, and a chill went down her back, which was thoroughly warmed. "There's at least four inches of snow out there now. You were frozen clear through, and your clothes—"

Morganna thought of the expensive camping gear she had purchased from the best outfitters. Her nifty canvas pants, layered with pockets, and her body-fitting silk underwear were especially chosen for the trip. Since the outfitter hadn't specified any rules about lacy bras and panties, she had chosen basic peach and black matching pieces. She guarded her secret fetish for the frothy bits of sheer lace with zeal. The man sharing his body heat with her would know her singular feminine weakness. She shuddered lightly as the image of his large hands removing her peach lace bra and panties skipped behind her lids. "My clothes?"

"They are damp. They'll stay that way until the sun comes out. This weather is supposed to last for days. You'll have to wear my dry ones."

"But you must be huge," she whispered, realizing that her feet rested on top of his and that his chin was tucked over her head.

"Big enough," he snapped. "And not all that happy. I suggest you quiet down and let me sleep. I'm a much better person in the morning when I've had a good night's sleep."

She fidgeted slightly, edging away and Jake groaned. "Will you stop that?"

"Why? I was merely getting comfortable." She bumped something hard and jutting and fought the wild blush rising over her cheeks. Her whole body went hot.

"That's why," he muttered tightly.

Fifteen minutes later the hard male body behind Morganna relaxed slightly and in another fifteen, the soft snore returned. She listened to the thump of her heart—the beat of his thudded slowly against her shoulder. Her stomach growled and she shifted. Her hip bumped his angular one and he started, muscles tensing. "Will you lie still?"

Morganna glanced at the boots near her face again. They were working boots...worn, and beneath the mud the leather was wrinkled.

He blew a strand of her hair away from his nose and shifted restlessly. His groan, though soft, boomed against the stillness of the meadow. His thumb smoothed her wrist in a caress and he groaned again, shifting abruptly away from her. "Damn," he whispered rawly, urgently.

"Yes, Mr...?"

"Jake. Look—for both of our sakes, you have got to hold still." He groaned again. "I'm not a happy man right now, lady."

"Well, then. It's your own fault. You shouldn't have decided to play the good Samaritan," she returned smugly.

He muttered something flat and succinct and flipped to his other side. The constriction of the bag drew her against his back, her breasts pushing against rippling, hot muscle. With one arm trapped beneath her and the other resting on his naked hip, Morganna squeezed her lids closed.

She drummed her fingers slightly on his hip, a habit she'd developed when she was concentrating on a tough business decision. Her stomach lay pressed tightly against his taut backside. "Ah...Jake. Yes, Jake. Ah...we're both...both completely naked, aren't we?"

"Hell, yes. Stop drumming those fingers on me."

"Oh...sorry. I do that when I'm considering something important."

"Consider this. I'm not a table top. It's freezing outside...maybe ten degrees if that—"

"How do you know that?" she asked, intrigued.

He groaned loudly, the sound loaded with frustration. "The limbs are cracking, breaking from the trees. An animal is walking on frozen grass, crunching it—a coyote maybe, foraging for food."

"Oh . . . right. What time is it?"

In an instant she was flipped to her back and Jake loomed over her in the darkness. She caught the line of high cheekbones and fierce eyes, his hair slightly long and brushing the massive shoulders that blocked out the night. "About four in the morning, and don't ask me how I know. You were freezing, Morganna. Even your underclothes were damp. Body warmth is the best remedy. I'm a pretty easy-natured man, but you are really testing the limits of my patience—got it?" He finished in a soft roar, his chest brushing her breasts.

The tips of her breasts tingled as she met his glare fearlessly. She was used to going toe-to-toe with her father's famed temper, and cowboys didn't frighten her a bit. But then she wasn't toe-to-toe, and the cowboy wasn't her father, and he wasn't wearing a stitch of clothing. Morganna blinked. "Ah . . . are we talking sexual interest?"

"You're a woman, aren't you?" he demanded between his teeth.

She flushed, uncomfortable with his close scrutiny. Men usually didn't notice her femininity in particular. They usually noted her power and bankbook balance, possibly her connections in the corporate ladder. "Morganna. I'm really tired. *Now* isn't the best time to discuss anything," he said too patiently.

"Yes, of course. I know that."

"Good. Now hold still and try to sleep," Jake ordered, easing her to her side and lying slightly apart from her.

Jake fought his aching body, riding it with iron control. Despite her recent hardship, Morganna Larrimore was neatly rounded in the right places, and he wanted her badly. She slept lightly, snuggling to him and draping her soft thigh between his. Awake, she was wiry, fast, but asleep, she was

cuddly and feminine. Her breast gently nudged his side as
she slept, and Jake realized that a bead of sweat had rolled
from his forehead. Her hand fell over his heart, the slender
fingertips drumming for a moment before Jake's hand covered hers.

He forced himself to doze and awoke to that small hand
drumming away low on his stomach. He was already
aroused when those busy fingers touched him. He jerked
away, wanting desperately to sink into that soft woman's
body and ease his desire. Jake curled his hands into fists,
willing his desire to pass. He ached in every muscle from the
tension, forcing himself to sleep.

He awoke to a flurry of activity, Morganna's tempting
body twisting agilely beside him, her legs tangled with his.
She was working furiously, muttering softly and jabbing
him with sharp elbows. Her bottom jiggled pleasantly along
his hip while she worked, then her elbow hit his eye. "What
are you doing?" he demanded, and realized that he had
shouted.

She continued working furiously, her bottom soft and
round against him, bumping him in erotic movements. "I
just can't seem to...the laces on this bag are fouled, Jake."

He closed his eyes and wished Morganna Larrimore into
another state. His body was aching, responding to those
pleasant little bumps of breast and hip and the intoxicating
scent of a woman's naked body. Shaking his head slowly,
Jake rubbed his chest where another elbow jab had scored.
"Morganna, may I help you?" he managed politely between his teeth.

"Well...uh...just a little bit more and I'll have it fixed.
The zipper is stuck.... I tried to move it awhile ago, and the
laces knotted in the zipper," she muttered. Jake grunted as
her bottom raised slightly, then settled on his stomach as she
sat. "I'll rescue us, Jake. I'm quite adept at knots."

Jake thought about the knots low in his body, his hand
tangling with her thighs, touching the silky triangle below
her stomach. He jerked his hand away immediately, looking up at the woman outlined in the faint light.

Concentrating on her task, her tongue touched her upper lip. He saw that Morganna was very pale with sleek, jet black hair that fanned smoothly around her head when she turned, then settled on her bare shoulders. Though she couldn't be considered a beautiful woman, character and strength lay beneath her Snow White complexion. Dark eyebrows winged high, and her lashes shadowed soft, flushed cheeks. There were generous, rosebud-tinted lips and a strong jaw, followed by a slender length of throat that he could wrap one hand around. In the dim light, one bare shoulder sloped into the full line of a breast tipped in mauve—Jake inhaled, grabbed the laces and tore them apart in one jerk. "There. Is that what you wanted?" he demanded roughly.

"Haste makes waste, Jake. I could have untangled them, given time," Morganna stated loftily and slid from his stomach to sit up, covering her chest with his shirt, which she had fished from a corner of the tent. "Now about those dry clothes. Where are they?"

Jake closed his eyes, willing his need away. He ached deeply to reach up, take the warm, soft woman's body in his arms and make love to her until they were both unable to walk. The thought startled him. He hadn't thought of making love—passionate, heated, mind-blowing lovemaking—since he was a youth foaming at feminine scents. In his adult life Jake had never unleashed the deep passion he suspected within him, carefully reining it with his wife. Morganna's soft body tested his patience and his passion, rocking the peace he had forged. "In the pack over there." He jerked his head toward a mound of bundles.

"Thank you," she said tightly, primly. "I'll have them laundered—I'll wash them when I'm finished. Now if you'll just turn around, please."

With a groan, Jake flipped to his side, listened to sounds of her foraging and found himself buried beneath clothing. He jerked a T-shirt off his head, slammed it against the side of the tent and asked in a quiet roar, "What are you doing?"

"Mmm. Choosing an ensemble for the day," she returned, digging furiously into his packs, careless of the clothing she'd strewn everywhere.

Jake stopped breathing in mid-breath. He'd never seen a woman so desirable as Morganna Larrimore, dressed in his boxer shorts and thermal undershirt and perched on top of mounds of clothing. He blinked and shook his head, then settled back to watch her dress in his jeans and a woolen sweater that dropped to below her knees. Those intuitive, slender fingers moved quickly. She couldn't stand, because of the tent's low clearance, but rather wriggled into the clothing, lying back to zip up his jeans. The motion revealed a smooth expanse of her stomach and Jake wanted to lay his hand over it.

For an instant he thought about those perfect white breasts he'd glimpsed while undressing her the previous night.

He wanted to lay his whole body over her.

Sitting upright, Morganna tried to roll cuffs into his jeans. He watched, fascinated, while her tongue crept out, her hands working furiously to fashion a wad of bulky cuff that instantly unfurled. Morganna began again, frowning with concentration. Her silky hair slid along her cheek, and Jake knew that the hairstyle cost more than his monthly feed bill. Those fast little hands fashioned two big wrinkled cuffs over her slender, pale ankles. Jake stared at her small, busy toes, which reminded him of the rest of her pale, agile body. The rush of sensual awareness startled him. She began tugging on his socks, which she pulled over the cuffs, then dusted her hands together briskly. "There. All through. Ready to start the day." She beamed at him in the dim light and sat with her legs crossed, giving him a good view of the wadded cuffs and the socks that came up to her knees.

Jake stared at the socks and closed his eyes briefly, fighting the urge to fold her cuffs. Morganna was a high-class snob who was used to butlers and maids helping with her clothing. He wouldn't play nursemaid to a dragon lady.

Then she grinned. A small impish grin, like a child who had just completed a major accomplishment. "The fresh air is invigorating, isn't it?"

Startled that he was thinking how appealing Morganna Larrimore was every time her breasts bounced and how he had better uses for the morning and the word *invigorating,* Jake glared at her.

Morganna studied the cowboy from beneath her lashes as she sipped hot coffee and huddled beneath his luxuriously warm down jacket. It smelled like smoke and leather, animal and a darker, exciting scent— She inhaled sharply and pushed away the tingling sensation running down her body. She concentrated on the huge breakfast he had cooked over the open camp fire. "When I start my fire, I'll fix you something to eat, Jake," she offered cheerfully, placing her plate aside. "The neighborly thing, you know."

He shot her a glare across the blazing fire, one straight black brow lifting high. "Fine."

She didn't like the sound of that word. As if he doubted her abilities. "Yes, well. I suppose I should get back to my own camp and get that big fire blazing. After that good night's sleep, I'll just wash my clothes in the creek and hang them up to dry. Maybe I'll catch a fish or two for lunch. Then I've got to repair my branch hut. You're welcome at my camp anytime, Jake."

"Fine," he said again in that same noncommittal tone. "I'll rest meanwhile."

Morganna stretched, feeling tremendously refreshed, then quickly grabbed for Jake's jeans, which were slipping off her hips. Jake looked away, his expression one of deep disgust. He lounged beneath the branch shelter, his long legs encased in worn jeans, and his stockinged feet crossed at the ankles. "Are you feeling all right, Jake?" she asked, sliding a bit in the snow as she trudged back to her camp. Her high, laced boots helped support the mass of denim at her calves. The bulky folds forced her to walk with her legs a distance apart. "I could feed the horses for you—"

"Don't come close to my livestock." He spaced out the words, glaring at her from beneath those straight black brows. When Jake's sultry, flashing eyes locked on her, the sensation of raging thunderstorms and lightning crashed over her. This morning his hair was mussed, probably by the many times he'd run his fingers through it. A sleek strand lay along his dark throat and she watched it lift and fall with his heavy pulse. Jake was very dark and big. Morganna estimated that he was almost a foot taller than her five-foot-five-and-one-half-inch stature. She had always resented that lack of height. In Kansas City she compensated with heels, a suit and a no-nonsense, brisk attitude. On a wintery mountaintop in Colorado, she refused to be intimidated by a tall, moody cowboy with eyes that shot out lightning bolts when he was angry.

"I understand why you consider the care of your animals a personal thing, Jake. Code of the West, or something like that? A cowboy always takes care of his own horse?" she asked, forcing herself to be pleasant.

He waved airily, then settled down to sullenly watch the flames. The mist hovered around him, a rugged man, obviously of Native American descent. His straight black hair touched the collar of his flannel shirt and his beard gleamed in the firelight. He closed his eyes, ignoring her. Poor dear, he probably needed the rest.

Morganna struggled with her sodden sleeping bag, attempting to carry it to a low-hanging tree branch. She worked quickly as she did everything, hauling great limbs from the forest to make her wonderful big blaze.

The raging stream tumbled by her, bouncing from rock to rock and preventing good fishing. She glanced back at Jake's camp, where a miraculous pot of something deliciously aromatic hung over the flames.

He was a beautiful man with a heavy growth of beard; his pose was timeless in the gloom. She blushed, remembering him naked and warm beside her. He seemed so aware of her as a woman. Freddie Mills and his college cohorts had been interested, though she later discovered their bet—who would bed "the ice Morg" first.

Morganna shook her head. Though the Freddie incident was years ago, she had discovered that few men could withstand her restless energy and need for challenges. She shot Jake a stealthy glance. He'd been aroused while they had shared the sleeping bag.

Not that Morganna had that much experience with aroused men. She had sidled away from the matter after a youthful expedition in the back seat of a classic Chevrolet, which had been parked at the side of a lake. The experience was quick and disgusting, something far better dropped in the lake and forgotten than cherished.

To push away her disquieting thoughts, Morganna alternately tried to meditate and build a better hut. Days ago her huge, multipurpose wristwatch, impervious to shock and water, had slid from her wrist into the stream; when she stopped to rest Morganna guessed the afternoon was well along. She assumed a meditating pose to disguise her fatigue.

She dreamed of beautiful, soul-quieting flute music circling the meadow, wrapping her in peace. The music floated around her, easing away her stress, and Morganna yawned, awakening slowly. She nuzzled her knees, absorbing the warmth, and longed for the children's tape she often played after a stressful meeting. She treasured that tape, given to her by Paul, who had acquired it from a sightless friend at a jumping frog match. It was so easy to drift on the music, letting it carry away the tension. She listened to the plop-plop of the rain falling in the forest and wished for a gooey, nut-filled, chocolate bar.

The appetizing scents from Jake's cooking caused her stomach to hurt. Mouth-watering scents clawed at her, despite her firmly closed lids. The sodden debris of her camp fire had rejected her last match, and the heavy layers of mist promised a cold night. She glanced at Jake's camp, lusting for warmth and food. He hadn't been in a good mood this morning for some reason. Perhaps his mood had improved throughout the day.

With Jake's help she could meet the challenge that her father had presented. In a better mood, Jake might listen to her offer. She shivered, her teeth chattering. And while Jake was listening, she would have use of his wonderful fire.

Wrapping the damp bag around her, she braved the rain and made her way around the huge puddle that separated their respective camps. It took all of her willpower not to snatch the freshly roasted rabbit and the beautifully browned squab from the branch over his fire. Steam lazily wound upward from a pot, and Jake lounged comfortably, sharpening his knife on a stone. A pot of coffee stood on a nearby flat rock, heating by the fire. Her peach bra and panties drifted idly on a rope to dry over the fire, lacy reminders of her current lack of underclothing. She wondered how to claim them with tact.

"Bear," he said quietly as she stepped into the light of his camp fire. "Big one."

She followed his stare to see an immense shadow moving along the brush near the creek. Morganna stepped closer and grabbed her bra and panties, wadding them into her jeans pocket. "Ah . . . Jake. I've developed a business proposal for you."

The huge hunting knife slowed for a minute, then resumed flashing rhythmically in the firelight. She noted Jake's long fingers, strong, yet tapered and artistic looking, contrasting his rugged appearance. She cleared her throat. "You see, I'm not the expert woodsman that you may think—" The knife slowed again, then returned to its steady pace.

He stretched against the saddle covered by a blanket and rolled his shoulders. "There's plenty of food. Sit down and we'll talk."

She gazed longingly at the roast squab and rabbit, the little flames that ignited when their juices fell. Her stomach hurt, aching for food. "Really, I couldn't. Perhaps when my campsite is better along, I'll be able to invite you to dinner."

"Suit yourself." He nodded, stretching his stockinged feet closer to the fire and wiggling his toes in the luxurious warmth. Morganna tried not to think of her damp, freezing ones.

Morganna needed to offer her proposal, needed his fire and the beautiful meat roasting on his spit. She swallowed and tried to sling her damp sleeping bag over a taut rope he had strung to the ground. The heavy weight shook loose excess water from the branches sheltering his campsite and a huge stream of water ran down on Jake's head. He jumped, ran his hand over his head to swipe away the water, glared at her and levered to a stooped standing position, looming over her. "Sit," he ordered, taking her upper arm in a firm grip and easing her to sit on a small box.

Jake crouched, grabbed her ankle and stripped off one muddy, boot, then the other. He tested the wet socks with a thumb running along her arch and scowled at her. Firmly placing her feet near the warm fire, Jake slashed a rabbit haunch with his knife, throwing it on a blue graniteware plate. He thrust the plate at her and jerked open a small tin near the fire to flip out a huge, fluffy biscuit, which he buttered and slapped on the plate. Jake ladled soup into a cup, plopped a spoon in it and placed the cup beside her. "Eat," he ordered, glaring at her while he resumed his lounging position.

Morganna hesitated the space of one second, her mouth watering. She tried to remember the proper etiquette for roast camp-fire rabbit—finger food or fork. She eliminated the salad and dinner forks, simply because none were offered. Daintily picking at the meat, Morganna stuck a juicy sliver into her mouth and closed her eyes, savoring the delicious flavor. Within seconds she was eating the other haunch and a second biscuit. The steaming soup was pure nectar, tiny bits of carrots and green beans floating in a barley-beef with onion base.

A scream split the misty night air and Jake sipped his coffee. "Cat. A big one."

"A cat, out here?" Morganna asked, wondering how such a small household animal could survive.

"Cougar. Wolves and coyote, too. This canyon is a favorite grazing ground of elk and moose. They've been circling all day, waiting for us to leave."

"You mean they've been out there this whole last week and a half?" Morganna's voice was high-pitched, squeezing through her tight throat.

"Those are bear marks on that tree at the edge of the clearing. Big cat marks on another not far from here. They're marking their territory against intruders. There's sheep sign on that rock slide over there. They've been waiting for you to leave."

Morganna eased a few inches closer to the fire and placed her plate aside, rubbing her fingers clean on the jeans she had borrowed. Jake's gaze skipped to the muddied knees. "Ah . . . when are you leaving, Jake?"

"I'm headed home at daybreak. It takes two days to reach my place."

"So you've finished hunting whatever you came up here to find?" she asked, and sincerely hoped he wouldn't murder a deer or any of the other nearby magnificent wildlife.

"Uh-huh." The rain began heavily after a brief pause and Jake reached beyond the shelter to toss her wet bag into the bushes. Once the weight was removed, the rope snapped back into place and a stream of water landed on his stomach. One big hand ripped across the flat surface, quickly swiping away the water while he stared accusingly at her.

Morganna concentrated on the fire and wrapped her arms around her bent legs. "I'd like you to stay, Jake, and help me set up an expert camp. Maybe show me a few things about foraging—" She frowned, glancing at him then the roast rabbit. "You didn't fire a shot today."

"Snared them. That big bear seemed edgy when you fired that shot over my head. He's probably had a taste of hunters and didn't like it. This is his ground. I respect his right to territory and gunfire can loosen snow slides or start a rock avalanche.''

''Bear,'' Morganna repeated hollowly and remembered the horrors of campers who had offended bear in some manner. She truly hoped she hadn't offended the carnivorous animal, or any of the variety of wildlife lurking in the pines.

''I'm not interested in staying, ma'am. Too dangerous. Just passing through and resting a bit. Thanks, anyway.''

Morganna studied the flames and glumly dismissed the beautiful campsite she wanted her father's private helicopter pilot to find. ''I see.''

She drummed her fingers on the cup she had been holding, then tried again. ''I could make it worth your while, Jake.''

When his left eyebrow lifted, Morganna continued. She'd developed several contracts and was an expert on labor negotiations. It was simply a matter of bargaining and patience. ''You see, there is a point of honor involved in this. My honor. I developed a plan to get away from the corporate structure, to bond with the other professional women on my team, to relax and meditate with them. They mutinied at the first drop of rain.'' She paused, forcing that edge of bitterness from her voice. ''As the CEO of my company—the chief executive officer—it behooves me to stick to my guns... to stay on the course that I charted. That is why I will pay well for your expertise...of course, you can't be anywhere around when the helicopter arrives... or let word get out that you've helped me.''

''Sounds good,'' he returned quietly. ''I could use the money. But there's one big hitch.''

Morganna tightened her grip on the cup and leaned forward. She badly wanted to show her father that she could succeed in what he had called a ''basically male venture.''

''A big hitch?'' she prompted.

''The late snow and the heavy rains have caused more than one death on Big Thorn mountain. It's a quirky mountain anyway, rock slides in the summer, pockets of thin earth where an underground stream has washed away solid ground. The face of that mountain—'' he nodded to a rock slide ''—came down when a hunter fired one bullet. The sound of a helicopter could shake loose a slide. Your pilot won't show until the weather settles down.''

"Oh," Morganna said bleakly, her fingers locked around the cup.

"Even if I wanted to take you up on that fat check, I've got to get back to my ranch. We're running shorthanded as it is. You could come with me.'' Jake shrugged one broad shoulder and looked at her intently. "Of course from the labels on your gear, your clothing, you wouldn't last longer than overnight without the luxuries a fancy CEO with a fat checkbook might have. You could catch the morning bus out from my place.''

Morganna's eyes jerked to him. "I am a business executive. I run a major company. What makes you think I wouldn't be able to cope?''

Jake's black eyes met hers over the camp fire. "Money doesn't cut it on my ranch. I don't cater to people who can't pull their weight. My ranch doesn't offer luxuries like butlers and maids. We work from dawn until night-fall...work hard. You'd wilt before nine in the morning. But you are welcome to stay overnight and leave on that morning bus.''

"I can't pull my weight? I'd wilt?'' she repeated, incensed, and drumming her fingers on the cup. She couldn't remember anything but overcoming challenges. She'd gladly work strenuous, long days with the satisfying reward of making her father eat crow. She squinted through the smoke. Jake Tallman would learn, as her father had, that she could meet any challenge. "Mr. Tallman, I can handle anything you dish out.''

For a moment those hard lips jerked into a brief, pleased smile, one that mocked her. "Is that a fact?''

Morganna's fingers drummed the cup. "Count on it.''

He sipped his coffee, nudging a piece of wood into the fire with his toe. His eyes skimmed down her, then back up.

"You'll change your mind. Like I said, we're running short on hands and there won't be anyone to baby-sit and fetch for you."

The beat of Morganna's fingers accelerated. Sprawled across most of the shelter he had created, Jake leaned his head against the saddle and closed his eyes.

The idea of mastering whatever one does on a ranch fascinated Morganna. She chewed her bottom lip and drummed her fingers. An expert at moulding business disasters into working, profitable concepts, Morganna itemized her options. Salvaging her pride was uppermost. She began to weave together the threads of a plan that could work to her benefit. If she could insinuate to those back home that this man came along and needed her help in some way, she could escape the deathly mountain—she thought of the bear and the cougar lurking in the pines who wanted to reclaim their territory. She really wanted to douse Jake's certainty that she couldn't manage on his ranch, and it was imperative that she save a measure of her dignity at Larrimore's. With regular calls to Rita—a trustworthy employee, though she had opted not to attend the primitive bonding opportunity—Morganna could keep tabs on the company.

"I've got to leave, Morganna," Jake continued softly. "This mountain is just too dangerous. If my trick ankle gave out—" He grimaced, stared at his ankle and let out a long painful sigh. "Too late . . . my ankle aches . . . it's going out. It may take a little longer, but I'll make it down okay. That is, if my ankle doesn't give out altogether."

"It is?" Morganna wished she hadn't sounded so cheerful. To rescue an injured man would be a wonderful reason to leave her camp. No one would question her lending a helping hand. Of course, she was sorry for his discomfort, but then she could ease his journey down the cursed mountain. With all the pieces falling neatly into place, she'd be a fool to let Jake and her opportunity to leave the bear-infested mountain slide by.

"Well, then, Jake. My reputation is based on my people-evaluating skills, and I trust your honesty. If you'll have me, I'm applying for the vacant job of that cowhand. I don't have my résumé with me, but my qualifications are highly rated on the job market. As a CEO of a major corporation, I'm skilled at logic and organization."

He opened one lid, then closed it. "We need someone to fill the gaps—help with the meals, clean around the house, feed the chickens—"

"A housekeeper?" Morganna leaned forward, excited at the prospect. Since her childhood, cooks never let her near the kitchen. She longed to bake all those wonderful things on television commercials.

"It's a fetch and do job. Feed the stock when necessary, run errands into town, things like that. There's only two of us, and we'll be working hard with spring planting, repairing fences and so forth. This next month is going to be the worst."

"I started at the bottom of my father's company in a 'fetch and do' job." She mulled the idea over. "Yes. I suppose the change of pace would serve the same purpose. To reenergize and stimulate, to refresh... Creative executives can suffer from burnout if they don't change paces once in a while.... Well, Mr. Tallman, it looks like we've just formed a partnership," Morganna said and stood. "You just take care of that ankle and I'll feed the stock. Ah...what do I feed them?"

"I can manage—"

"But your ankle needs rest." She began rummaging beneath the tarp covering his packs only to have her wrist swiftly snared. His skin was very dark against her slender wrist, his long fingers gently firm.

"Not my stock," he said in a tone that resembled a growl. "I can manage that."

Morganna understood about cowboys bonding with the horses, but she really wanted to see the beautiful, big horse and mule up close. She wanted to make friends with them so that when Jake's ankle gave out completely, they would follow her orders. It never hurt to create a backup plan. Perhaps she could make a stretcher across two poles attached to his horse, place Jake in it and drag him to safety. She'd seen a *travois* used in movies and longed to create one; however, since Jake wouldn't let her near his animals, her masterpiece was squashed. Slightly miffed by his exclusive animal rights, she stood very straight and nodded. "Fine. Then it's settled. I'll be ready before dawn. My campsite will be cleaned and everything packed away. They recommend that, you know, leaving nature the way we found it. You just lie there and take care of that ankle. I'll take care of you."

She wanted to prolong returning to her camp and leaving Jake's warm, dry one. The sleeping bag inside his tent would be wonderful. She tried to prevent the sneeze tickling her nose, and Jake studied her carefully. "You could take much better care of me if you'd stay nearby, Morganna," he said evenly.

Frowning, she debated for half a heartbeat. He was openly asking for her help. How could she refuse? she thought cheerfully. "That is very good logic, Jake. I'll just go tidy up my camp and bring my things over here for packing in the morning. I'll sleep out here, of course. Intruding on you for one night was enough."

His stare was shadowy, dark and oblique. A muscle jerked beneath the skin covering his high cheekbone, and his large hand curled tightly around his cup. "You take the sleeping bag. I'll sleep out here."

Morganna remembered the sleeping bag and Jake's hardened body that morning. She turned slightly to hide her blush. "Nonsense. I will not have concessions because you think I'm a helpless woman who must be coddled in the wilderness. As an intelligent, contemporary woman, I resent any partiality because of my sex. Then there's your weak ankle, and the chill won't help it."

She resented his steady stare and that one lifted straight eyebrow. "We'll both sleep in the tent," he amended in low, carefully spaced words. "You won't be much help to me if you catch pneumonia."

She hated Jake's obvious and correct logic. She drummed her fingers on her thigh and wondered if the bear and the cougar would decide to reclaim their territory before she evacuated it. Though she did have her pistol, she really didn't want to kill a potential mother or father of any wildlife species. "True. Though I am perfectly comfortable with sleeping outside the tent, maybe I'd better keep an eye on you. People develop fevers from injured bones and muscles. You may need me . . . you take the bag and I'll manage quite nicely nearby."

"Nearby?"

Morganna cleared her throat. She'd never slept beside a man—other than Jake the previous night. The thought was disconcerting. Her nasty habit of talking in her sleep could be dangerous. He could discover how badly she wanted to leave the mountain. Or that lately she worried about time running out on her biological clock. "I'll sleep beside you. Outside the bag. Inside the tent. That way when you wake up and need anything, I'll be able to hear you."

When he nodded slowly, watching her, Morganna stepped out into the night and began dragging her camping gear to his camp. After two trips, she was thoroughly exhausted. When she discovered that Jake had retired for the night, she dropped to the log in his branch shelter and untied her boot laces. Her cold, damp fingers shook, and she extended them to the fire. A bucket of steaming water sat on a flat rock, and a towel and a tiny bar of soap waited nearby. A huge clean flannel shirt and a pair of cream-colored thermal bottoms were neatly folded beside the towel.

Tears sprang to Morganna's lids. She pushed them away impatiently with the back of her hand. Injured as he was, Jake was thoughtful for her comfort.

"Ohh!" she cried delightedly, finding hot water in the coffee pot and a tea bag in one of Jake's huge cups. Instantly Morganna forgave his hogging of the animals' care.

Three

Jake crouched beside Morganna's sleeping body. In the heavy fog of early morning, the animals moved restlessly, sensing that they were heading home to a warm barn and dry hay. Only the tarp that had served as the floor of the tent, the sleeping bag and Morganna Larrimore's tempting, restless little body remained to be packed.

He realized darkly that very little kept him from climbing into that sleeping bag with her. All he needed after years of striving for peace, of pushing away memories, was to have this woman strip away the veneer he had guarded for a lifetime.

Jake wanted his fierce passions kept captive and secret. He wanted his heart untouched from more pain. The woman lying near him threatened him, threatened what he wanted....

Jake scowled down at the top of Morganna's head, which was all that could be seen. Tossing restlessly beside him throughout the night, Morganna had talked in her sleep. He'd gotten a running insight of a corporate woman who resented a good night's sleep, who demanded profits in the third quarter and who worried about her brother, Paul. Then there was "Daddy," "Father," "checkmate," and a rolling, threatening dialogue about the mutineers sprinkled with the word *keelhauling*. After a half hour of her muttering and tossing, Jake had jerked down the zipper of the bag and eased her into it. A mop of wet hair had hit him in the face.

Now his finger stroked one gleaming strand. Damp with the fog that swirled around the meadow, her hair was essentially dry. Last night it was wet from her shampoo and Jake had grimly dried it with two towels while she muttered in her sleep and squirmed against him for heat. In the end his muscles ached and Morganna's busy, slender fingers added to that tension. Unable to sleep, he rose an hour earlier than he had planned, left the tent and promptly stepped on Morganna's expensive camping gear. For the last hour he had unfouled the tangled mess, packed the animals and listened to Morganna's mutters about "a matter of timing . . . everything fitting in nicely with my plans."

Jake breathed slowly, watching a strand of that silky black hair. When her body curled into a ball, the strand slowly slid down into the bag. He resented how his body reacted to Morganna's soft one, how after years of celibacy, a spoiled, dedicated-to-profit female tyrant had jerked him back into realization of body needs.

A true opportunist, Morganna was using his "injured ankle" as an excuse. He would remember to limp occasionally, but playing on her sympathy was too easy. She'd taken the bait like a hungry trout, disregarding the danger in camping and traveling with a man she didn't know well. Remembering a woman hiker who had been molested by an unknown assailant last year, Jake frowned.

The gleaming, silky strands pushed slowly to the top of the bag, then her face emerged and a delicate hand, palm upward, lay beside her head. Those slender, tapering fingertips continued moving. A sheaf of bangs slid across the fine black eyebrows; her lashes fanned down across her cheeks. Jake's eyes narrowed when he studied her mouth. Slightly parted, her lips looked lush and warm and inviting. She stretched and yawned and smiled sweetly in her sleep. Jake doubted that few people saw Morganna smile. He shrugged aside the small shadow of guilt for misleading her. Dragon ladies were known to bite when offended.

Inhaling sharply, Jake shook her shoulder. He didn't want to feel that tug of tenderness for a woman who looked innocent yet provocative in her sleep, and who became a living steamroller when awake. "Morganna. Wake up."

"The television hasn't come on yet. I'll just wait for the news," she returned sleepily, turning on her side toward him and snuggling contentedly into the bag's flannel lining, her eyes closed. "Put out my gray pinstripe suit, will you, Mavis? I'll want the morning paper with my broiled grapefruit and whole wheat toast. Just a few minutes more, then I'll be awake and waiting when the tray is ready."

Jake fought the smile tugging at the corner of his lips. Morganna would learn a few necessary lessons before he was finished. Obviously well tended by others, she had neglected the courtesy of cleaning her dirty dishes or folding and packing the mess she'd made of his clothing the previous morning. His fingertip prowled down her sleep-flushed cheek, noting the pale, delicate texture. She sniffed, wiggled her nose and fluttered her lashes, opening her eyes slightly. They widened instantly, then she scrambled out of the bag, standing on it while she stared down blankly at Jake, whom she had knocked to the mud.

He got up slowly, towering over her while he brushed off his sodden backside. She yawned and stretched, his flannel shirt opening to reveal the deep crevice of her breasts. Jake shook his head and closed his eyes. Dragon lady or not, Morganna Larrimore was a curvaceous, full-fledged disaster, and his body jerked to attention when she moved, which she did constantly. The thought that he was barely a notch above a teenage boy nettled him. He handed her a plate filled with biscuits, liberally buttered and spread with jam, then thrust a coffee cup into her hand. "Your pinstripe suit is at the cleaners," he stated between his teeth.

"Hmm?" Morganna sat, her legs crossed, devouring her food. Jake watched, fascinated by that bit of clinging raspberry jam on her bottom lip. His height allowed him a view of her breasts. They were pale and beautifully curved, just right to fill his hands—Jake swallowed. Abstinence and propinquity were not reasons to take Morganna on that bedroll, no matter how tempting she was at the moment.

She looked up at him and grinned brightly. "Goodness. It's a lovely morning, isn't it?" She frowned, tilting her head, the tip of her tongue flicking to that bit of jam. "Is something wrong, Jake? Oh, it's your ankle, isn't it? You must be in pain."

Jake jerked down the wide brim of his hat. He tossed fresh clothing on the bag, nodded once, turned and walked to the dead camp fire, which he began cleaning away. Thrusting against his jeans, his pain wasn't in his ankle but ranged farther north and required shielding from Morganna's curious green eyes. Through the years he'd met and known a number of sweet, quiet, calming, intelligent women. None of them had reached inside his gut and fired his desire like this frustrating woman, whose energy wreaked havoc to system and logic. He had created a life of peace that suited him. His desire for Morganna's pale, agile body trespassed on that studied calm.

"Oh...Jake...." She called behind him. "Ah...isn't something missing in my ensemble? Ah...underclothing?"

He turned to find her stomping around on the sleeping bag with her muddy boots, searching the folds. In the next second Jake lifted her from the bag and plopped her in Black Jack's saddle. Two seconds later he had folded and packed the bag and swung up behind her on the saddle. Her hair struck his cheek as she turned to him, her eyes bright with anger, her cheeks pink with the flush that rose from her throat. "You don't need to manhandle me, Jake. I did take riding lessons."

Jake stared at her—the cause for his taut, aching body...the reason for his sleepless nights. He pressed his lips together, refusing to respond. She glared up at him then, with those flashing emerald eyes, and said, "I don't see what your problem is, Jake. I am helping you out, you know. *You need me.*" Then she smirked, and Jake sensed that dangerous little lifting of her mouth could cause strong men to shudder.

"Don't push me," he warned tightly, sliding his arms around her to take the reins.

She didn't blink, her expression impassive and her shoulders set rigidly. "Are you threatening me, Mr. Tallman?" she asked, very softly, dangerously.

Jake looked down at that pale face with its expensively cut hairstyle, which was smooth and shining without brushing. The furious challenge in her eyes taunted him. Then he was bending to her mouth, taking it almost roughly, his hand cupping the back of her head. The kiss was meant to silence her effectively, to threaten and to trim a measure of his raw emotions toward her. He absorbed the soft explosion of her breath, sensed the tightening of her body and tasted the sweetness of her incredible mouth as it softened, lifting gently toward his. The fog shimmered around them, cool against his skin, her mouth warm and inviting. Jake found himself kissing her tenderly, tracing the firmly closed line of her lips with his tongue, while one arm caught her close to him. He heard the soft sigh, her body leaning toward his, her hands clenching his arms.

She tasted like heaven, sweet and new...like wild, hot passion lying just beyond his reach. Hungry now, Jake changed the angle of the kiss, drawing her against him. Her mouth was hot and yielding, her breath striking his cheek with an irregular beat.

Then thunder rumbled in the distance and Black Jack shifted restlessly beneath them. Jake ended the kiss reluctantly, slowly, nibbling and easing away until Morganna's eyes slowly opened. The green shade had shadowed mysteriously, her lips moist and full in her pale face. She trembled within his arm, leaning back against it to survey his expression. "That was uncalled for, Mr. Tallman," she said huskily. The soft tremor that ran through her body rocked him. "It won't happen again."

Then with queenly dignity she turned, straightened her shoulders and waited for the trip to begin.

The muscles in Jake's face ached, the pulse in his throat throbbing with frustration and the need to kiss her again. He scowled at a badger darting through the underbrush. He had never taken a woman's mouth roughly, and realizing that Morganna could cause him to act rashly didn't help his unsteady nerves. He wanted to sink into her and forget everything but that soft, warm body.

By early afternoon Jake learned that he preferred Morganna's excitement and exclamations about the beauty of the mountain's wilderness; her stealthy glances and silence unnerved him. Morganna Larrimore kissed like a warm, willing innocent with an incredibly sweet mouth that he wanted to teach and devour. The knowledge increased Jake's dark mood. Morganna Larrimore was, by her father's admission, not soft and sweet. She argued like a dragon lady and showed tendencies of being a miniature dictator. When he refused her suggestions for different paths down the mountain, Morganna had bristled and accused him of being "pigheaded."

Jake also found that she was tough and a natural athlete, evidenced by her scramble up a treacherous ravine and the bubble of laughter signaling her success. Enchanted by the wildlife, the mountain sheep, deer, squirrels, who stopped to watch them pass, Morganna squirmed around for better views and once almost unseated them.

When they stopped at a clearing to rest the animals, Morganna slid from the horse. While Jake tended a scratch on Pinky's flank, she disappeared. Jake cursed, ran his hand through his hair, then spotted the sole of her boot beneath a thicket. In two strides he reached her, grabbed her ankle and pulled her out. When she aimed a ladies' defense chop at his head, he bent and plopped her over his shoulder.

Shivering with anger, Morganna struggled and lashed out at him. "I'm sure there were edible mushrooms in that thicket, Jake. Foraging provides food for the camp fire, you know. No one has ever dared treat me with such . . . such obvious lack of respect. If your wife puts up with this caveman stuff, she needs psychiatric help."

Jake's long stride to the animals stopped, his thoughts racing. He had never used force with Dianne, always gentle even in their sexual play. The woman on his shoulder created havoc with his inner peace, and he realized suddenly that he had never treated another woman like Morganna. The thought stunned him as he eased her to the saddle and swung up behind her, taking the reins. "My wife is dead. So is my son."

"Oh." She glanced curiously at the grim set of his jaw, expecting him to continue.

With the experience of a man who shared little, Jake refused to enter into further discussion.

"Oh," she said again, something darting in those quickly veiled green eyes. "I've never tried parenting or marriage, but it must be devastating to lose someone you love. I am sorry about your family."

Jake inhaled sharply. He didn't want this woman exploring his past, nor his future.

Morganna was silent, then she took a series of short naps in the late afternoon, her face tucked beneath his ear. Each movement of Black Jack brought her parted lips bumping gently against his lobe and Jake's body had developed an ache that promised to be permanent.

He wondered what perversity had caused him to want her breasts free while they shared the ride, why he had jammed her bra deep in that expensive duffel bag. Though covered by layers of clothing, the soft weight enticed him with every step Black Jack took.

By nightfall, Morganna was certain that Jake's trick ankle was worse. She awoke from a power nap—a segment of no more than fifteen minutes—to find him holding her tightly, his forearm a heavy weight beneath her breasts. When she looked back at him, he was scowling, tiny beads of perspiration shining on the stubble covering his upper lip. She patted his arm. "Don't worry, Jake. I'll see you through this rough patch," she assured him, frowning when he groaned softly and closed his eyes.

She regretted those firmly closed lids, for his eyes were wonderful, jet black and framed by straight black lashes, a reminder of his Native American heritage. They were expressive eyes, signaling instant temper, deep quiet thoughts and that blaze of unrecognizable emotion when he had looked at her. Morganna shivered, her body in tune to Jake's hard one. She mentally flipped through magazine articles she had read concerning protocol for impending lovemaking, the who-does-what-to-whom firsts.

The moment Jake stopped in a clearing and said, "We're making camp tonight here," she scooted out of the saddle. Anxious to help she began tearing at the expert knots Jake had tied in the mule's pack and succeeded in loosening one. All of the bundles plopped heavily to the wet ground, forcing her to jump back.

"What are you doing?" he asked. Hearing the words above her head, she turned and bumped into his chest. It was a very wide chest, his shoulders blocking out the dim light filtering through the tall pines. With a dark look he said, "Get back and don't move. Don't touch anything."

Desperate to prove that she was not entirely helpless, Morganna began helping to set up the camp the moment Jake tied the tarp over the horses.

She moved quickly, dragging the bundles away from the animals and separating the tent. She pushed away the kiss they'd shared, refusing to debate the sweet aching tenderness that it had begun. Jake could kiss very well, despite the rather fierce onset. She studied his long frame as he chopped wood.

Jake had tasted like passion, a heady fierce emotion swirling around her before the kiss had changed into a nibbling, tender hunger. The fiery exchange excited her, and she probed the short back list of men she had kissed. They paled beside Jake's virile western image, and Morganna delved into her own stirring passion. A dynamic woman who actively pursued her business needs, she couldn't picture herself as a passive partner in lovemaking. The male back list crumbled into dust when presented with equal opportunity in passion. She appraised Jake's tall, muscled body and decided that it could withstand an energetic assault.

During the day, she had considered revising her list of potential candidates for the father of her baby. She wanted a baby before her biological clock ran out. She had considered an arranged marriage with a business peer or having affairs, but none of the candidates really seemed that appealing. Most of them wanted either her money or her power. Jake, however, wanted neither of those things. Once he lost his suspicions about her ability to cope on the ranch, he would be more receptive to parenting her baby. Then she wanted to examine him closely under pressure, in day-to-day living experiences, before asking his input. Instantly Morganna pictured Jake's dark body against her pale one and blushed. Her stay at his home would be an excellent time to thoroughly research Jake as potential parenting material.

All in all, things were working out nicely. She had escaped the dangers of primitive solo camping, acquired an expert woodsman with an injured ankle who needed her help. She considered Jake's long-legged western stride and decided that his ankle must have temporarily mended. She blushed, remembering his naked body next to hers and the warm hard muscles rippling around her. They felt unbelievably wonderful next to her freed breasts. She swallowed hard and fought the trembling warmth inside her body.

Morganna unlashed the packaged tarp that served as the floor of the tent and considered Jake. While he spoke little and seemed prone to dark moods, Jake could be trusted . . . like when she lost her way on another little foraging expedition, and he had come for her. There was a certain roughness in the way he'd picked her up and plopped her on that massive beast. The noise of his grinding teeth when he had mounted behind her had been unsettling for a moment.

He was tasty. Some perverse feminine particle of her being delighted in those dark, dangerous looks as though he'd wanted to—she flushed—well, make love with her. Morganna's eyebrows lifted with surprise. That look was desire...passion...*for her.* The startling thought stopped her drumming fingers. From the latter part of his kiss, she sensed that Jake would be a tender, thoughtful lover, though she wasn't certain if her body would accept his large one easily. A tiny quiver raced along her lower stomach when she thought about sharing the tent with him again tonight. Jake's arousal had boosted her feminine ego, which she had tucked firmly away since her early twenties and that awful skirmish in the back of the classic Chevrolet.

Then Jake was towering over her, glaring down at the tent heap. He shot her a look of disgust and began setting up the cooking fire. In the dry tinder, the tiny flame sputtered and flickered and Morganna squatted to blow on it. It sputtered and died, and Jake pressed his lips together firmly. The muscle running over his cheekbone instantly developed a small tick. "Sit down, Jake. You must be in pain. Please let me help you. You'll need your strength for tomorrow," she offered as he relit the fire with a wooden match.

"Morganna," he said heavily, wrapping his big hand around her neck gently. "I want you to rest. Put your cute little bottom on that log over there and sit still until I tell you to move."

"I wouldn't think of it—" she began only to have him bend and place a hard, fast kiss on her parted mouth. Then he looked down at her and scowled darkly, as if he resented his actions.

When Morganna recovered, she was seated on the log he had indicated and running her fingertips over her lips, while Jake established the camp and began cooking. *Cute little bottom* wasn't a term used for the Larrimore Corporation's chief executive officer, nor was it a term any man had applied to her derriere. Positive now that Jake was a sexist, a chauvinist and a macho Tarzan-type all rolled into one, Morganna resented the implication that she couldn't handle her responsibility to Jake and his trick ankle. She drummed her fingers while he concocted something in his pot, heated water and brought her a cup of tea. She resented how easily he maneuvered her with that mind-blowing kiss. "May I move now, Mr. Lord of the Mountain?" she asked as he walked the few paces back to the camp fire.

Jake stopped in mid-stride. His tight smile wasn't nice. "I'll tell you when. Sit there until I do."

After dinner he ordered her to the tent. Resting on top of the sleeping bag because she was uncertain of who slept where, Morganna watched with fascination while Jake's shadow on the tent wall stripped and bathed. Her fingers drummed on the cup of tea she had been nursing, and she realized her lower body had suddenly moistened. She flipped to her stomach, overheated in Jake's flannel shirt and thermal pants, and took several long breaths while she counted to twenty.

"What are you doing?" Jake asked, easing her into the sleeping bag despite her protests.

She began to sit up and he pushed her shoulder down easily, settling in beside her. "Why are you in a snit?"

Morganna wondered how she could trust a man who moved silently and handled her with such ease. She lay rigidly on her back, her shoulder touching his side. While she was fully dressed, she remembered his preference for à la nude. "Ah . . . Jake, are you wearing clothing?"

"Shorts," he explained after a huge yawn. When he stretched, a hard arch of male beside her, the sleeping bag shrank.

She resisted the urge to curl up to his wonderful heat. "Do you really think it necessary that we share this bag? I could sleep comfortably outside."

Beside her Jake breathed quietly, his heat curling around her. "Morganna, have pity. I am an injured man after all. A very tired one. Sharing this bag is just the simplest way to keep warm and dry," he said softly in that low, sexy voice he rarely used. In fact, Jake really didn't talk much at all. He used his eyes and hands to converse, and she'd noted how easily he managed the animals with those big, calloused hands and long, skilled fingers. She was still awake when Jake began to breathe heavily, his body relaxed in sleep. Then slowly Jake curled around her, spoon fashion, and cuddled her against him.

Lying very still, Morganna swallowed her tiny gasp when Jake's easy breath swept through her hair. "Blossom," he muttered and then his large hand was cradling her breast. Morganna barely breathed, debating her next move. Jake's thumb swept across the tip of her breast and she inhaled sharply, and closed her lids as desire quivered through her. Jake hauled her close, nuzzled her hair and settled down to sleep with her breast in his hand. Through the flannel, his palm was very warm and gentle, carefully enclosing her breast as though it was precious.

An animal cried out in the night and Morganna forced herself to lie very still, dissecting her emotions. After fifteen minutes or so, she decided that Jake made a wonderful sleeping partner. She rather liked that big, firm hand gently cupping her breast and placed her own over his. In the morning she would find out why he had called her "Blossom."

Jake's morning moods weren't pleasant, she discovered. He slapped her backside, which was covered by the sleeping bag, and shoved a cup of coffee beneath her nose. Fully dressed, he had the animals saddled, packed and waiting, while she dozed blissfully in the open, mist-layered meadow. Morganna glared at a chipmunk who eyed her from the steadily dripping underbrush. She sat up carefully, shoving away the hair from her cheek when Jake draped his jacket around her shoulders. He hesitated, then carefully lifted her hair from beneath the collar, smoothing it gently. He tossed a bag of dried fruit in her lap and crouched beside her, studying her intently. "This isn't going to work, Morganna," he said carefully.

The dried apricots melted in her mouth. "Why not?" she asked around the delicious bits and wondered how to haul him back into the bag, trapping him like the famous spider and fly. Jake was too big to play the fly. He captured her drumming fingers, holding them gently.

"If you stay with me—helping out at the ranch, we'd be living in the same house."

Determined to succeed, Morganna clambered to her feet. The sack of dried fruit tumbled to litter Jake's boots. He looked at them and closed his eyes. "Take my word for it. You'd better take that offer of the morning bus off my ranch. I'll send your gear."

"I will not leave. I am helping you off this mountain and proving to you that I can manage at your ranch. Don't forget you need that extra hand, Jake," she reminded him triumphantly. "Your ankle could give out again at any time." Few people changed the rules when she was involved, and she wanted a better glimpse of Jake as the potential father of her child. She had met challenges all her life and she didn't intend to start wimping out now.

When Petey pulled the pickup and horse trailer to the base of Big Thorn Mountain late that afternoon, Jake wanted to lift the shriveled, ageless little cowboy and kiss him on the lips. Anyone who could rescue him from Morganna's incessant questions would have received the same treatment. He wasn't used to snapping at anyone, nor the surly way he felt, nor the way he wanted to take that sassy mouth beneath his. To keep her busy, he had allowed her to add wood to the fire. The smoke from the wet and green wood rose slowly, a signal for Petey to make his pickup.

Petey circled the battered truck, his squinty eyes leveled at the small figure pulling, pushing and fighting huge limbs to cover the tiny, smoldering fire. Morganna had insisted Jake rest his ankle while she tended the signal fire, and he had spent that time surveying Morganna and keeping the fire alive. When she fell on her backside after a limb gave way, Jake cursed Nathaniel soundly. The maniac probably had been driven to insanity by this same determined woman.

"What is it?" Petey asked, his weathered, lined face shrouded beneath the battered western hat. He studied Morganna, dressed in Jake's bulky clothing and began moving toward her. "A boy? You found a boy up on that mountain top? Some runaway? What?"

Jake decided to let Petey experience Morganna first hand. He led the animals into the trailer while Petey cautiously approached Morganna. She turned suddenly and Petey's scrawny rear landed in a mud puddle. The small cowboy churned to his feet, his fists raised, and Jake yelled quickly, "Petey! It's a woman!"

The small cowboy jerked off his hat, swatted it against his bowed legs and turned to scowl back at Jake in disbelief.

Petey's scowl and bad mood remained while Morganna sat between them in Jake's dark green pickup truck, surveying the sprawling fields and cattle. Gripping the steering wheel, Jake tried to ignore her drumming fingers, which had somehow settled on his thigh. He shifted, then allowed his hand to rest over hers, stilling it. Morganna's eyes darted up to his as she blushed and slid her hand away.

"A business executive," Petey grumbled. "You run a company... a female chief of staff," he repeated carefully. "A woman."

"Larrimore Corporation. I'm the CEO," Morganna returned absently while she scanned Jake's small house. "Jake needed my help to get off the mountain, and for the next month I'll be pitching in at the ranch, doing odd jobs."

"Boss? Larrimore—that's the name of the guy..." Petey's eyes shot to Jake who shook his head. "I...uh...think I've heard the name...uh...boss? *You* needed help to come off the mountain?" he asked cautiously.

"His trick ankle was acting up and he needed me," Morganna explained smugly. She leaned forward in the seat, searching the old barn and the log and rock house with its wooden shake shingles and sprawling front porch. "Oh, Jake. It's the prettiest house I've ever seen," she whispered, her face lighting as she turned to him, then back to the ranch. "Oh ... chickens and those cute cows with the white faces and stocky red bodies—"

"Herefords," Jake informed her, aware of Petey's eye slits widening as he stared at the woman between them.

"Uh ... boss, where's she going to bunk? I'm not sharing no house with no prissy female and there's only two bedrooms, anyway."

Morganna's silky hair fanned out from her head as she pivoted to Petey. "Me? Prissy? I'll have you know that I've lived in major cities all over the world and coped with mobsters and magnates alike."

"Magnets? Like the kind that stick to refrigerators?" Petey asked blankly.

Morganna took a deep breath and settled back with her arms crossed over the jacket Jake had loaned her. "You'll see. I intend to succeed. I was an immense help to Jake on the way down. He needed me."

"I'm bunking in the barn, boss," Petey muttered, eyeing Morganna warily.

"No, I will. I've never asked anything of others that I wasn't willing to do myself," Morganna shot back.

"You're sleeping in the house," Jake interrupted, stopping the truck in front of the barn. He wanted Morganna where he could watch her until Nathaniel located the man who had threatened her. Jake tossed an incentive at her, "We haven't completely gotten rid of the rats and mice yet. Petey can cope better than you can, though there's no reason for him to move out."

"Blasted rats bit off a cowpoke's nose once on a ranch south of Denver," Petey muttered crossly.

"Rats? Mice?" Morganna suppressed a shudder, her face paling in the shadowy light. "Call the exterminators!" Her voice rose in panic and Jake noted with satisfaction that she had eased closer to him.

For all her steely executive business nerves, Morganna demonstrated that she trusted him. Trapped between guilt and passion, Jake gripped the steering wheel and hoped that Nathaniel was making progress in the case.

"One of the rats was bigger'n a cougar. Carried off the traps and ripped 'em apart. Scared the cat away," Petey informed her gleefully.

"Well...uh. Then, of course. Jake, do you mind if I use your telephone to inform my people that I am fine? I'll need some of my things, too."

Jake didn't want any trails leading to his ranch. "I knew you couldn't make it without your luxuries and that bank-roll," he challenged. "You've got plenty of clothes—too many. If you need anything, there's a general store in town. You could live off your wages, which you haven't earned yet."

Morganna glared up at him and firmed her lips. "Yes. Well, of course I don't need anything extra...I'll just call my father and my most trusted assistant. Rita can manage the details with my direction."

Jake thought of how worried Nathaniel really was and nodded briefly. When he got a chance, he would tell Nathaniel just where he could go.... "Fair enough."

Later Petey smoothed out the wrinkles on the cot in the barn and sat down, lighting his hand-rolled cigarette. He squinted at Jake over the spiraling smoke. "We haven't had rats since we moved in eight years ago. So what's the deal, boss? Why did you bring her back here? When did you get a trick ankle, anyway? She's spoiled rotten. Probably wants champagne for breakfast. I've heard tales of female executives," he added warily.

Jake finished oiling the saddle, turned to Petey and briefly outlined Morganna's danger. Petey tossed out some lament about when the West was man's country, and females stuck to their righteous places in the kitchen and the bedroom. When Jake entered the house, he tossed his hat to the peg on the wall and stared grimly at the soapsuds bubbling from the closed washer, the messy kitchen and smoke pouring from the oven. Clothing and the pack bundles were strewn throughout the spacious kitchen and living room. The open door to his bedroom revealed that a tornado had gone through his chest of drawers, clothing tossed carelessly aside and hanging from open drawers. Jake ran his hand through his hair. He wanted to place that hand around his guest's slender, vulnerable neck and— "Morganna?"

"In the bathroom, Jake. I've started the washer, and your dinner is in the oven. See? I'm helping already," she called airily. "Lovely little get away you have here. . . . I hope you don't mind, but I'll have to use a few of your clean clothes until mine come back from the laundry. I've already put some things in the washer and called my father. Just put my luggage in whatever room you want me."

By the time Morganna emerged forty-five minutes later, Jake had cleaned the kitchen, finished the laundry and was sitting staring at his fire, contemplating the errors of his ways.

At the slight sound of the door opening, Jake turned to see Morganna's hair wrapped in a towel, her body covered by his T-shirt and loose boxer shorts. Her legs were bare down to the bunched folds of his socks. His worn flannel robe dragged on the floor as she made her way to him.

Fresh from her bath, Morganna excited him as no other woman had. While he had acted gently, tenderly with his wife, he wanted to toss Morganna to the couch and— The thought enraged him and he jerked to his feet and pointed to the bathroom littered with clothing and towels. "Get yourself back in there and clean up!" Belatedly, he realized he had shouted. He resented how easily she could ignite his temper, when the whole countryside recognized his patience.

Morganna's eyebrows lifted. She stared at him coolly for a full second, then turned slowly to the bathroom. She turned back to him. "Take a note, Jake. No one ever—repeat, ever—raises their voice to me. I just don't tolerate it, even from my chauvinistic, overly traditional father. You must be under pressure of some sort. Is your ankle hurting?''

Jake took a step toward her, and to his satisfaction Morganna's eyes widened and she stepped back. "Uh…is there a problem I've missed, Jake?''

"You never clean up after yourself, Morganna. If you're staying here, you pull your own weight and that includes cleaning up your own messes,'' he almost roared. He snared the front of her T-shirt and robe in one fist and drew her slowly to him, lowering his head to glower down at her. While at the time, he couldn't prevent himself from wanting her savagely, he intended to control the order in his home. "Clean it up. Now.''

Undaunted, Morganna's green eyes met his evenly. "You've been chewing on something all day, Jake. Surely the matter of a few damp towels isn't enough to make such an issue. Take your hands off me, please,'' she ordered in that imperial tone.

"Fine,'' he returned tightly, releasing her slowly. He wanted quiet, his fire and no Morganna Larrimore, in reverse order.

"I didn't realize it was such an issue. You seem to be forever packing and cleaning—''

"I am since I met you,'' he returned darkly with the odd sensation that the only thing that could ease his tension was to sink into Morganna's pale, sweet-smelling, agile body. "Get used to taking care of yourself. Look around. There isn't a butler, a housekeeper or a maid within one hundred miles. We do for ourselves, and we don't ask others to do it for us—got that?''

Angry with himself, Jake resented the way Morganna could raise his emotions. He'd pasted his life back together after a disaster and lived in moderate peace and quiet. The threat to his peace shivered inches below his face, and Jake pressed his lips together, resenting the image of a bully that he now portrayed.

"Oh, of course," she said in a small voice, her eyes glancing at the bathroom. "Yes. I..."

The robe flurried after her as she ran back to the bathroom. Jake closed his eyes against those long, enticing legs. He shook his head slowly, then eased onto the couch and lay there, watching the flames in the fireplace.

Nathaniel had better work fast.

Four

Morganna ignored the rooster's crow and the ray of sunshine wheedling at her firmly closed lids; she could not ignore the second heavy swat on her backside, though the heavy patchwork quilt softened the blow. "Morganna, wake up," Jake ordered in whip-cracking tones.

While she refused to open her eyes, Morganna said very softly in her best threatening CEO voice, "If you brutalize me again, Mr. Tallman, I won't be responsible and *I will retaliate.*"

"Lady, that is a challenge that is hard to pass up," Jake murmured before he scooped her up, quilt and sheets, carrying her to the breakfast table and deposited her in a chair.

Petey sipped his coffee and eyed her suspiciously. "She's not gonna make it, boss. Pampered piece of female city folk," he stated sourly and forked two huge brown pancakes on her plate. "Buckwheat. Sticks to your ribs and puts hair on your chest." The little cowboy glanced at her and reddened, then said quickly, "Boss and me have already eaten. There's chores waiting."

She met Jake's expressionless stare and blew a strand of hair away from her hot cheek. She wanted to launch herself at him and pay his swats back in spades. She had never physically attacked anyone before, and the prospect that Jake could evoke such primitive emotions outraged her even more. "I owe you," she said evenly, threateningly, dismissing how wonderful he looked without his beard. His skin was bronze, shining along his jaw, and she ached to place her palm over that itsy bitsy cut on his chin. She wanted to place her tongue on it and lick— She glared at Jake who was watching her with interest. "Count on it."

"You're scaring me," he returned easily, then sipped his coffee. "Sleep well?"

She hid the instant flush, averting her head. Dreams of Jake's hand caressing her breast and savoring his hungry kiss didn't leave much time for sleep. Then there were images of his beautiful, lean brown body and some confused flash of herself, à la nude, riding that muscular body. In her heavy fatigue, she'd probably confused Jake with Black Jack. Her body heated and she frowned, avoiding Jake's intent look. The look held and darkened and Morganna realized her breasts were aching slightly. She blinked and in that instant the image of her riding Jake flipped over, his dark body now covering hers. Straightening in the protective wad of quilt and Jake's robe, Morganna buttered her pancakes and shot him threatening glances while she ate the delicious, grainy cakes. She wondered how Jake liked the canned corned beef and noodle casserole she had prepared last night, then decided against asking him. With liberal seasons of salt and catsup, a little lemon juice and cayenne, it was delicious and healthy despite its unappealing look. "What's on the agenda today?" she asked, studying the warm, cozy home fully for the first time.

The sunlight danced along the windowsill, sliding onto the beautiful hardwood planks of the floor, broken only by heavy, braided rugs. Varnished logs lined the room, and a huge wooden chest, topped by an old, wide-framed mirror stood against one wall. A rocking chair and a long, wood frame couch covered with a woven cotton blanket in a Native American pattern sat in front of a massive rock fireplace and an old-fashioned rocking cradle rested in a shadowy corner. A glass-covered gun rack, filled with powerful rifles, dominated a corner, and a black, rotary telephone perched on a scarred oak desk.

Morganna noted the heavy, serviceable primitive furniture and the three large, covered baskets lined against one wall. The predominantly dark woods and barren decor lacked a softening touch of plants, framed pictures or personal mementos. The huge kitchen spread into the living room, and the sparse furnishings were very neat and organized. The scarred plank table was sturdy and long, and the sunlight caught on the pottery salt and pepper shakers, the huge crockery pitcher filled with milk.

An iron pancake griddle sat on top of the small gas stove's burners, and a huge white package rested in a granite wash pan beside the sink. A small room for coats and boots angled from the kitchen. A mismatched automatic washer and dryer stood beneath stacks of towels and her neatly folded clothing. A gigantic chest-type freezer dominated the room.

"After you do the dishes and put your things away, meet us outside," Jake said as the men stood. "Make your bed."

Morganna stared at the mounds of dishes, cups and the huge bowl crusted with hardened pancake batter. "Dishes," she repeated hollowly. She had never washed dishes in her life, although she had placed her late night milk glasses in the dishwasher out of respect for the cook. "There are so many."

Petey grinned nastily, jerked a bottle of detergent from beneath the sink and tossed a wet dishrag at her. He nodded to the large package in the pan. "You can start the roast in the oven before you come outside."

Jake stared down at her, and for just a minute she hoped that he might rescue her, then he inhaled slowly and jerked on his hat and was gone.

Determined to show Jake exactly how she could manage under primitive circumstances, Morganna slid the wrapped

package and granite pan into the oven and turned on the
heat. She plunged into the dishes, and placed them all on the
rack to dry. She dressed in record time, selecting one of her
nifty, new canvas trousers with lots of pockets and a sweater.
She threw the covers back on her bed, shoved her clothes
into the primitive oak dresser and hurried out into the clean
country sunlight. Inhaling the chilly, damp air, she stretched
luxuriously and stepped off the wooden porch. She would
bond with nature, relax and meditate, take long contem-
plative walks and refresh—

A huge, striped and heavily pregnant gray cat squalled
when Morganna stepped on its tail. The cat streaked across
the barnyard, startling Black Jack. The Appaloosa whinnied, reared on his back hooves and Jake fought to stay in
the saddle. Morganna froze in mid-step; the huge animal
and Jake were outlined against the sky. Jerking the reins
hard, Jake managed to pivot the horse, and those massive
hooves hit the ground a full yard away from her.

Petey ran out from the barn, carrying a bucket of milk.
He tripped over the cat who was nursing its injured tail. A
good measure of milk was spilled before he recovered his
balance. Before Morganna could apologize, Jake's large
hands lifted her up in front of him. "Stay put," he ordered
sharply, encircling her waist with his arm, while his free
hand reined the horse. When she turned, she met his thun-
derous stare and decided perhaps she would debate the
matter of his hauling her about later.

"I apologize. Accidents happen," she explained tightly as
Black Jack pranced around a flurry of big red chickens. A
rooster squawked and Pinky brayed.

"Lady, *you* are the accident," Jake said grimly, drawing
her close to him. His jaw slid across her temple, his breath
uneven against her skin.

Jake dismissed Petey's startled "Well, I'll be a—" The
terror pasted on Morganna's white face when Black Jack
had reared close to her would last a lifetime, and he wanted
her tucked close against him, safe from harm. He slashed a

dark look at Petey, who had tipped his hat back and placed his hands on his hips. The cat, Curds, exacted her payment for damages by licking from the pool of spilled milk.

Morganna stiffened in his grasp, and he drew her tighter against him, his hand flat on her stomach as Black Jack pranced out of the ranch yard. The rural mail carrier, Hugh Blanchard, slid by on the county road passing Jake's ranch. Hugh leered from the shadows of his four-wheeler's cab and took his time driving away.

Dipping his hat to the postman's big wave, Jake concentrated on keeping Morganna's agile body against his own, despite her protests. With a madman stalking her, Morganna needed to know her territory, and Jake pointed out landmarks on his ranch. Nettled because of the way he had reacted to her danger, Jake extracted his revenge by curtly ordering Morganna to help him check and repair fences. When her eyes blazed back at him, her body stiff with defiance, Jake discovered that he liked testing her patience as she had his. Amusement replaced his raw nerves, and once he pushed a smile away from his lips.

Along the way, Dirty, a half wolf, half German shepherd, found them, sliding out of the pines and keeping his distance. Dirty would never be fully tamed, already a young adult when Jake extracted his paw from a trap. A companion in loneliness, Dirty kept coyotes away. In the winter, Dirty took refuge in the barn, keeping the rodents at bay and acting like a puppy when Tyree Lang stayed for a few days.

"Jake! There's a wolf," Morganna cried, turning in Black Jack's saddle to look behind them.

"Dirty has been following us for ten minutes," Jake returned, then noticed that the dog was acting strangely. He turned Black Jack, and the dog loped off. "He wants us to follow him."

"Dirty?" Morganna repeated the name.

"Because he looks dirty. He's half-wild, but a good dog. Keep away from him."

Dirty led them to a burned, ragged tree that had been recently struck by lightning. Two of Jake's prime cows and their young calves had died with the bolt. Black Jack danced, uneasy with the scent of death, and Dirty sat a distance away, watching the humans.

Jake worked furiously, piling brush and limbs around the dead cattle and Morganna worked with him. Wrapped in his frustration at the loss of good cattle by a freak of nature, Jake didn't notice Morganna's tears until he lit the fire and stepped back. She stood apart, her fists balled at her side, refusing to give way to the tears that slid slowly down her cheeks. Looking small and vulnerable against the backdrop of the rugged pines and soaring mountain range, Morganna bit her trembling lip. Her eyes dared him to note her softness. "Nature," Jake explained roughly, unused to comforting or being comforted.

"Yes," she whispered unevenly, a little of the defiance crumbling. "They were so . . . so beautiful."

Jake looked away quickly. He wanted to tuck her against him and never let her go, to kiss away the tears shimmering in her soft, green eyes. The fierce need frightened him, lodged in his trembling hands. Pain lurked around caring too much, and Jake had spent years building a barricade against the tender emotions.

When she tossed another branch into the fire, Morganna winced and Jake snared her wrist. He carefully reached for the other and turned her palms upward, already suspecting the scratches he found there. Morganna tried to draw her hands away and Jake fought the tenderness washing over him. Taking care, he slowly drew her hands to his face, kissing away the pain. Her fingertips trembled on his cheeks, and Jake gave way to the need to draw her into his arms, to shelter her from the pain. For just a moment, she didn't resist, lying quietly in his arms, then she sniffed, and Jake tucked her face into the hollow of his throat and shoulder, holding her tightly. "I am not crying," she whispered huskily. "Oh, Jake . . . they were so beautiful."

Too dangerous, he thought distantly . . . too dangerous to care for a woman after all these years. Not this woman, and not now, when his life was finally tolerable.

A silky strand drifted along his jaw, and he lowered his face into her hair, unwilling for the moment to draw away, protecting his scarred heart. With this woman's scented warmth and soft body came a danger he could ill afford.

Distrusting his tangled emotions, Jake lifted her carefully and placed her on his saddle. They rode quietly back to the ranch, and he found Morganna's hand gripping his arm as if she needed him. Jake fought the wave of pain surging through him as he laced his fingers with hers. Keeping Morganna's scent close, by nuzzling her hair, Jake closed his eyes when she leaned slightly against him, resting for a time.

The tenderness grew, swirled around his heart, tugging at him. When they reached the ranch yard, Morganna slid to the ground and swiped the back of her hand across her eyes. He wanted to ease her pain and remembered the "bottle-feeders" that Petey had collected from another rancher. Bottle feeding the calves was a task Jake enjoyed, and somehow he wanted to share this bit of tenderness with her. Inside the barn, the four small Hereford calves instantly clamored for milk when they saw Jake. Morganna's expressive face lit up. "Oh, Jake, they are beautiful," she exclaimed, reaching through the slats of the pen to rub their noses. "Oh, look at him, he's adorable."

"That's a heifer, a female, Blossom," Jake murmured, standing close to her. His hand curled into a fist, his mind and heart fighting that gentle, dangerous tug.

To take her into his arms was too easy, too treacherous.

When Morganna turned, tears glistened in her eyes and she dashed them aside. "I am not crying," she stated hotly, and Jake watched, enchanted as her bottom lip quivered. "Don't think that I am, because I am not...."

In the late afternoon Morganna stacked wood outside the house, her hands protected by his leather gloves. Jake watched Petey stand on tiptoe to stare out the kitchen window at her and fan the smoke away from the burning paper and roast. Jake inhaled deeply and dialed Nathaniel's private number. "Jake," he said simply when Nathaniel answered.

"My daughter called last night. Apparently it was necessary for her to leave her comfortable campsite and beneficial meditation to help you down the mountain. I find that hard to believe, Jake, and what's more she says that you need help for the next month or so. She's worried about Paul, my son. Seems she thinks I mentally brutalize him," Nathaniel muttered. "Then she has already called an assistant, checking on progress of her various projects, though she didn't tell them her location— That's dangerous, Jake. You've got to keep her away from a phone. Those calls could be easily traced," Nathaniel stated flatly.

The haphazard woodpile that Morganna was building leaned slightly, and Jake asked, "Have you got any leads?"

"I've got a team on it. They'll turn up something."

"I'll check in. Right now your daughter is in danger of being buried beneath the woodpile."

The woodpile began sliding slowly, piece by piece, just as Jake wrapped an arm around Morganna and jerked her back from harm. "That's gettin' to be a habit, boss," Petey remarked lightly beside him and began calmly stacking the pile again.

Morganna shook free and jerked down her jacket. "It certainly is. Here I was, minding my own business—completing a task you assigned to me, might I add—when suddenly you are hauling me around like one of those bales of hay."

Jake looked at her sassy, soft mouth and thought where he'd like to haul her... beneath him. The thought startled him and shooting her one last threatening glare, Jake swung around and walked stiffly toward the barn.

That night Morganna trudged past Jake when he opened the door, slid off her jacket and dropped it to the floor. Easing out of her pullover sweater, she let it slide to the floor on her way to her room. "I'll have a bath and dinner in that order,'' she said after a huge yawn, then loosened and kicked off her boots. ''Wake me in an hour.''

Petey shook his head and continued rewashing the dishes Morganna had rinsed that morning. Jake stripped off his gloves and placed his hat and denim jacket on their proper pegs. ''We eat at the same time, Ms. Larrimore. Or not at all.''

Morganna stopped, pivoted slowly and walked back to Jake. Those widely spaced, clear green eyes met his. ''I'm tired, Jake. I didn't have a chance for a power nap today, and I usually take at least three in one day...depending upon the amount of pressure I'm facing. I find that it keeps the mind at its best.''

''Fine. Take your nap. The next meal is breakfast.'' Jake washed his hands in the sink and ignored Petey's nudging elbow. The scrawny cowboy was showing signs of weakening. Morganna approached the table, studying the juicy, salvaged beef roast and mashed potatoes. A smudge of dirt ran across her cheek, and her eyes were dark with anger and fatigue. She glanced at the apple cake cooling on the counter and the bowl of whipped cream beside it. There hadn't been time for lunch and Morganna hadn't complained. He watched her expressive face, watched her weigh hunger against pride, and square her shoulders. Her green eyes slashed up at him, brilliant with anger. ''You're enjoying this, aren't you, Mr. Tallman?''

''You won't make it,'' Jake taunted softly, watching the pink flags of color rise in her cheeks. With a madman stalking her, he had to keep her locked to him with whatever means available. He resented the protective emotion she stirred and the desire that wouldn't cool, leaving his body tight and aching. ''There's always the morning bus out.''

She arched one delicate brow and ran her fingertip around the rim of a blue granite dinner plate. She tapped it lightly. ''If it interests you so much, you may take the bus out.... You know, I've never wanted to physically attack anyone in my life, Jake. But right now, I'd love to wipe that smug look off your face. I am not a quitter.'' Giving him one last meaningful look over her shoulder, Morganna went to the sink and washed and dried her hands, then sat at the table.

A taut silence settled over the meal. Gradually Morganna's eyes drifted closed, her head nodding sleepily. "Boss?" Petey whispered, when Morganna's head finally settled to her chest.

Jake inhaled sharply. He didn't want to hold that tempting, curved body against him. *He didn't want any part of the danger of caring too much. He especially didn't want this female dynamo reaching into his life and jerking away the safety he had studiously built, hour by aching hour.*

With the sense of a man clinging by his fingertips to the edge of a dangerous volcano, Jake slowly, grimly allowed the air in his lungs to escape. "Boss?" Petey prompted again, looking at Jake curiously. "You got indigestion? Was the roast that bad?"

"She's driving me nuts," Jake admitted before he realized he'd spoken.

Petey removed the fork from her hand and wiped away a drop of whip cream from her lip. "Yeah. She's one of those challenging females. Kinda reminds me of a kitten in a way, though. Spitting mad one minute and cuddly the next. She's the kind who could keep the right man on his toes."

"Uh-huh," Jake agreed grimly. Taking care, he lifted her into his arms and found Morganna's face nuzzling the side of his neck. Her mouth on his skin caused a hard tremor to race through him, and he discovered himself gathering her closer as he walked to her bedroom. He wanted her in his bed, safely tucked beside him. The images of her pale body and that sweet untutored kiss were endangering his sanity.

When he returned to the kitchen, Petey winked. "She's gotten to you, boss. The days of slidin' away from women and charmin' at the same time are gone. This little lady isn't the kind to allow you to play the lonely wolf. You'll be dancing to her tune soon enough."

The little cowboy chuckled when Jake leveled his best deadly stare down at him.

* * *

At six o'clock the next morning, Else Murphy's battered truck barreled straight toward his house and pulled to a stop. Morganna huddled in her quilt on the kitchen chair opposite Jake, glowering at him. "I am not a happy woman now, Jake," she stated darkly. "No one has ever dared to jerk me out of bed like you did a few minutes ago. You're lucky you're still in one piece. I do have several courses of women's self-defense behind me, you know."

"Your behind is staying put," Jake returned easily as he gripped his coffee cup. He watched Else's happy grin shining behind the muddied windshield as she prepared to get out.

Else and Morganna converging in his house on the same morning was frightening. The chemistry between the two energetic, plotting, headstrong women could defeat an army of kamikaze fighters. Jake settled down in his chair, readying for the explosion. His chances for peace and survival were sliding downhill by the second. The quick image of himself battered around inside a pinball machine by two highly charged women fanatics flew across his mind. He didn't like the little trickle of fear that raised the hair on the back of his neck.

"My 'behind is staying put.' That sounds suspiciously like an order. I don't take orders," Morganna shot back, her expression defiant.

"Learn." Jake leveled his eyes at her, half hoping she'd disobey. Unused to dealing with frustration, Jake now faced Else and her basket of family recipes—jams, breads and homemade butter. He also faced huge dollops of maternal advice and the sparkle in Else's eyes. He'd skimmed by his cousin's matchmaking attempts for years, but her grin foretold disaster. Jake found he wanted to make Morganna pay for his fallen kingdom, the breach of his security. While Morganna inhaled sharply, he mentally ran through the logical sequence of events to prompt Else's visit.

Yesterday Hugh, the rural mail carrier, had spotted a woman sitting in front of Jake on Black Jack. Hugh's wife promptly called Else Murphy, the oldest Blaylock sister. Else's mother, Elizabeth Blaylock, mother of the huge family had tracked Jake to a home for wayward boys. At fourteen Jake had already experienced a round of foster homes, and for a time he resented Elizabeth plopping him in the midst of the lively, loving family. Elizabeth taught him that "family was family, and blood ties were stronger than steel." Jake was a second cousin to her sons, and by that right he was perched beside her family in the church pew every Sunday and attended every family "do." Elizabeth had whacked him with her wooden spoon just like her sons when they forgot to treat a woman properly. The entire Blaylock family wrapped him in love, and after the first disquieting months, he loved them back.

Else had inherited Elizabeth's wooden spoon along with the privileges of being the matriarch of an extensive and powerful family. Bearing the height and dark coloring of the Blaylocks' Spanish, Apache and sturdy pioneer blood, Else wore her mother's earrings. Those pearl earrings combined with Else's dressy slacks and sweater set, rather than her usual work clothes, signified that she intended to wield her matriarchal prod.

She found Morganna sitting glumly in the kitchen, wrapped in a quilt and studying her coffee with a dark, seething look. Fascinated with Morganna's brewing temper since he'd scooped her up and plopped her at the breakfast table minutes ago, Jake sipped his coffee. Else, a tall, angular woman, was a sharp contrast to the softer, paler Morganna, who was now glowering at him. When he moved to stand, his cousin pushed him down.

"Jake. Beautiful morning, isn't it?" Else asked, placing the basket on the counter. She unpacked an assortment of jams and homemade breads while sliding looks at Jake and Morganna.

"Mmm." Morganna drummed her fingers and shot a dark look at Jake, who settled back to wait Else out. She'd come for information, and he didn't like that speculative sparkle in her eye.

"So..." Else poured herself a mug of coffee and sat at the table. "It's a standoff, is it?" she asked mildly.

"That..." Morganna nodded to Jake and huddled deeper in her quilt. "Is a brutal man. One I shall enjoy destroying. I will find his weak spot and disintegrate him."

"Mmm." Else sipped the coffee she had poured into a mug and grinned at Jake. "So this one isn't exactly falling for your charming manners and good looks, hmm?"

"Lay off, Else," he ordered gently. "Morganna Larrimore, this busybody is my cousin—"

"And mentor. Sometimes I have to remind Jake of a few basic facts of life," Else interrupted sweetly. "The outside lines of your telephone have come loose in the storm, Jake. Though I tried to call yesterday and the line was busy."

Jake inhaled slowly, grimly. Disconnecting the telephone seemed a simple way of keeping Morganna's communications to a minimum. "Thanks. Else Murphy. She ramrods the whole Blaylock family and considers me one of her lifelong challenges. Now that she's married off her brother, Dan, she's been picking on another one, Rio, and myself. Don't get any ideas, Else. Morganna isn't my type."

"Mmm?" Else murmured, turning to Morganna who was glaring at him.

"You didn't do a good job trimming Jake's manners, Else," Morganna stated flatly, her green eyes flashing at him. "The strong, silent, lord-of-all-he-surveys type is out of mode in today's world. Women prefer a man with emotions—" She glanced uneasily at Jake, and licked her lips and Jake found his eyes locked to the moist inviting tip of her tongue.

"Mmm. Strange. Jake is usually so polite. So charming to women...while he's backing away, hoarding himself out here," Else murmured. "Strange," she said again, thoughtfully.

"He's a physical, dominating brute," Morganna continued, glaring at Jake. "He's always tucking things away. Folding and tucking, that's what he does. Then there are those dark, moody looks. He has a terrible temper."

Else's brows jerked higher, and she turned her head to Jake who said tightly, "Morganna has agreed to help. Her maid and butler stayed at home." Jake fought the effect of no sleep and his desire for the woman, who was staring sullenly at him. Morganna was a restless sleeper and every time her bed creaked, he thought of other uses for that uneasy, creamy body and those creaking springs. He resented the way his body ached for completion in Morganna's.

"He picked me up bodily this morning—*and* yesterday morning, and deposited me in this chair. He calls me 'Blossom.' No one ever calls me anything but my given name."

"Ah! I see," Else cooed sympathetically. "Why don't you go along, Jake, so we can talk?" she asked lightly.

Morganna's lips moved, fashioning that tight, dangerous smile. "Yes. That's a marvelous idea. Why don't you run along, Jake?"

He glared at the two women, found Else's cocky grin and Morganna's narrowed, challenging eyes. Their invasion was successful. Retreating and wound licking was his only option. "Fine. I'll talk to you later, Else—before you leave." Jake rose, jammed on his hat and walked stiffly out of his house, currently infested with gossiping women.

An hour later, Else stepped into the barn. He didn't trust her easy, impish smile. "Life's great, huh, Jake? You've hid out here, acting like an old wolf, hiding from life, and guess what? You trip right over it."

"Lay off, Else. Morganna is here for a reason."

"Oh?" His cousin smiled knowingly.

Jake explained grimly, and Else's beaming expression slid to one of concern. "I hope they get that guy soon. Stalking a woman like that is sick, and Nathaniel was wise to tuck her away for the duration."

Uncomfortable with his part in tucking away Morganna, Jake jerked down a harness and began slathering polish on it.

Else petted one of the calves. "In the meantime there's no reason for Morganna not to enjoy herself.... There's a dance next Saturday night. Don't you dare keep that girl away from Jasmine's Spring Do. I'm the head of the committee and I want everything to be better than last year. You turn up in a pleasant mood and make sure Morganna has a nice time. There's enough Blaylocks around to keep her safe. By the way, that girl needs jeans and I'll send some out with Hugh. He's dying to make a delivery to your door. Right now the whole town thinks you've gotten married. It doesn't seem very gallant to expose a nice girl like Morganna to gossip and speculation. One story has it that your sexual pressures built up, drove you crazy, you got drunk in Denver and got her pregnant."

When he leveled his best leave-me-be scowl at her, Else grinned. "I knew it would happen sometime. She's just what you need, Jake. A sweet little thing just won't do for you now. You're stirred up and she's the reason, if you admit it or not. You've had things your way too long."

Her expression softened, her hand gentle on his cheek. "You pushed away what you were to survive, Jake. When you're a child and darkness crosses your path, it takes a lifetime to recover. Then a second tragedy locked your heart. You stripped yourself of anything to do with Dianne or your love, Jake, and you've worked to mend the hole in your life. She'd want you to go on living and loving. It's really time to stop hiding from happiness. Mother would want you to have everything. She loved you—we all love you so much."

Though Jake knew the family considered him as theirs, Jake had seen enough of Else's matchmaking and was wary of her high percentage of success. The thought of her and Morganna united in any way caused him to shiver mentally. "You know what your mother meant to me and the whole family. But I'm managing just fine now without you stirring up trouble, Else. If you're trying to pay me back for the time I put that lizard in your bed, pick another way."

"Times change and people change with them. You treat that girl right and no telling, I may just see you become a father. Give life a chance. Give that girl a chance. There's no denying the sparks flying between you. Attraction is a wild animal, Jake. It runs free and can't be tamed, nor can the heart. You loved Dianne in a gentle, true way. I suspect that Morganna is tempting passions that you haven't explored. I've always thought that you shielded your heart from everyone. You are an artistic, passionate-natured man, Jake, and you've fought that nature your entire life. Maybe it's time you started to live. Don't be frightened. Loving hurts and it gives."

"Else, you mean well. But let things be."

"This one isn't going to let your good looks and charm send her on her way, dear cousin." She patted his shoulder. "Try some flowers...maybe a nice dinner in town. Poor thing, she's been fighting to hold her own in her father's world, trying to prove that she can equal Nathaniel's nonstop, high performance. She hasn't had time to be a woman, Jake. For all her business knowledge, she's really sweet and innocent." She elbowed him gently. "I'll bet she kisses that way, too."

"You've been busy. She probably didn't recognize your spy techniques. And for your information, I know the protocol for dating," Jake informed her flatly and shifted to conceal his blush. He truly hated it when Else tortured him, jabbing away at things he wanted hidden and laying them at his feet.

Else's grin widened. "It's been a long time. You may have forgotten a few things. Though I understand that you shared a sleeping bag with her to keep her warm." She laughed outright. "That was nice, Jake. You were a perfect gentleman. I'm proud of you."

He inhaled, scanning the cool, hazy peaks of the mountains rimming his ranch. While Else plotted away, he had other plans. "Once Nathaniel has the situation under control and locates the man making threats on Morganna, she's gone."

"She's the sticking kind, Jake. The kind that meets every challenge that's tossed at her and deals with it and herself in the best way she knows how. I like her," Else answered quietly.

Five

A few minutes after Else zoomed away in her truck, Morganna stood behind him. "Your cousin was very informative, Jake." He continued to crouch and bottle-feed one of the four thirsty baby calves, while Morganna circled around him to stand against the wall of the barn. "One of my people skills is exacting information without the person's realizing they are being interviewed, you know. You have some good points," she said thoughtfully and began to pace back and forth in front of the hay bales.

Jake decided instantly that while Morganna was interviewing Else, his cousin was finding out the facts and laying out plans. "Else has some misguided idea that you are a kind man...a thoughtful man wounded by the world and hovering around like some sort of—like Dirty—without a kind touch to tame you. By the way, she's invited me to the Jasmine Spring Do and I wouldn't miss it, with or without you."

Eager to waylay him, Morganna had apparently dressed quickly. As she moved, the missing buttons of one of his flannel shirts revealed her pale peach bra. Jake suddenly remembered the soft breast it covered, his mouth tightening against the fierce desire ricocheting through him.

Morganna threw out her hand. She leveled green, furious eyes at him. "I, on the other hand, know a different side of you. Jake Tallman, you are not nice. I've decided to cross you off my list of possible baby makers."

While Jake fought the nudging calf and the emotional hot potato Morganna had just tossed at him, she continued undaunted, "You need my services too badly for me to leave promptly. But the minute my month is up—*hasta la vista*, Mr. Tyrant."

"Baby maker?" he asked slowly, placing aside the bottle and stepping outside the calves' pen. He ripped off his gloves and tossed them aside, walking to Morganna slowly.

Her eyes widened. "Well...ah... Just a slip of the tongue, Jake...uh...." She cleared her throat. "Ah...forget I said that—"

"Baby maker," he repeated slowly, aware that no other woman had ever touched his temper or his primitive emotions like Morganna. He advanced a step and noted with satisfaction that she stepped back. "Yes, that would fit in with the dragon lady image—select a likely candidate—some unsuspecting— Me, hmm?"

Backed against the wall, Morganna inhaled sharply, exposing the exciting, pale curve of her breast. "It won't work. Just one of those imaginative concepts that are a trademark of my style...well, sometimes my concepts just don't jell . . . like now, for instance."

The idea of making a baby with Morganna startled Jake, tempting him, while the woman standing before him could raze his carefully constructed peace with a sweep of her slender hand. "There's romance, Morganna. Kisses. You can't have me without that," Jake murmured, placing both hands beside her head. He lifted a silky strand with his thumb, letting it slide along his tanned hand and studying the contrast. "So. Does the scenario run like this? Locate a likely candidate, propose a deal to him—oh, but you haven't asked me, have you? What were you going to do? Stay long enough to get pregnant, then take that bus? Would you tell me if you had my child?''

The sweet image of Morganna's curved body sheltering his child ripped into Jake's heart. He wasn't prepared for the tenderness, the possessive emotions washing over him. The thought of another man producing Morganna's baby caused a hot wave of anger to hit him. Then she caught her trembling lower lip in her teeth and Jake reeled with the taut desire riding him.

Her eyes darted to his mouth and away. ''Jake, I've already discounted the idea. No need to worry. You're off the list.''

''List?'' he repeated dangerously, tracing the shape of her upper lip, one he wanted to nibble. ''You put me on a list of possible baby makers?''

She swallowed, the blush rising up her cheeks fascinating him. ''Well... there was the list of potential husband material and you didn't qualify....'' she explained limply. ''I... would want someone less... less dominating, someone more in the standard corporate figure—'' She shot out a hand in a futile gesture.

''Well?'' Jake had his fill of plotting females for the day. This second assault on his life-style was too much. If the challenge was tossed into his lap now, he might as well defend his territory. Tormenting Morganna might ease a measure of his frustration.

He watched with interest while Morganna floundered, blushing wildly. Jake framed her cheek with one palm, noting the contrast of dark, callused fingers against her ivory complexion. He stroked her cheek, brushed the delicate corner of her mouth with his thumb. ''It's nice to know you considered me proper material for one list, anyway. No doubt you have a careful little list of qualifications and you were going to wield your people skills to determine if I qualify. Do you know that you are restless at night, Morganna?''

When she shook her head, he asked, "Do you have any idea what the sound of those all-night, creaking springs does to a man? Especially a man who remembers every inch of your bare skin laminated to him in a very snug sleeping bag? You're a restless woman, Blossom, and I wonder if there are better ways to spend your energy." With that he bent to nuzzle her hair, inhaling the fragrance. Tenderness had replaced the rocketing desire. The need to stroke and hold Morganna until she heated tugged at Jake. She blushed wonderfully, enchanting him, and he was startled to find himself smiling gently, teasing her. "Blossom, you don't even know how to kiss and there's a whole lot of mileage between kissing and baby making."

"Of course, I do—" Jake placed his mouth carefully over Morganna's, something he'd wanted to do for two days. He nibbled the soft startled "O" of her mouth and slowly, carefully drew her body against his. She was soft and fragrant and very hungry, Jake discovered. He sank into the kiss, gathering her closer, his hand stroking her back and lower, following the soft curve of her hips. She stood on tiptoe, pressing against him, her hands cradling his face.

Taking care, Jake deepened the kiss, teasing the closed opening of her lips gently. "Open for me, Blossom," he whispered huskily, aware of her heat enveloping him.

He was tasting her, soothing her, gently destroying her defenses, and Morganna wrapped her arms tightly around him, keeping him close. Flowing through her fingers, his hair was sleek and warm. His thighs pressed against hers, his hard body vibrating with a fever she didn't understand.

Then the hunger took her, racing, heating, searching for the answers Jake promised with his kiss. She was flying, held tightly in his arms, lifting, straining to meet his mouth.

Tenderly, carefully, Jake slowed the kiss, easing the hungry tempo and stroking her gently. He held her to him, her cheek resting over his racing heart. He swayed with her in his arms. "Shh . . . Blossom."

Forcing her fingertips to release his shoulders where she had been clinging, using his strength as a lifeline in the sweet desire, Morganna trembled and ached. She shivered as the cool air of the barn touched her hot cheeks. Jake's thumb caressed her cheek, his dark eyes tender and mocking.

Morganna closed her eyes and trembled, a fresh tide of desire ebbing over her. Through a throat tightened by emotion, Morganna managed unevenly, "So. You can kiss. Big deal."

With that she summoned her unsteady knees and forced them to walk her away from Jake.

The day stretched into night and Morganna hadn't had one power nap. The memory of Jake's lips kept her energized. She'd been held and cuddled and tasted tenderly, sweetly, then in hunger. Her fingers drummed the quilt, and she refused to move. In the living room Jake paced quietly, and Morganna watched the shadow of his feet pass the lighted crack under her door. She inhaled, then watched his shadow pause for a long minute in front of her door. "Jake?" she whispered, aching for the sweet possession of his kiss.

"Go back to sleep," he answered after a moment's hesitation.

"What was she like, Jake?" she whispered and waited, listening to the silence. His feet moved away, and Morganna waited, realizing that Jake barred the past from her as securely as the closed door. Wrapping the worn robe around her, Morganna entered the living room to find Jake standing before the fire, running his hand slowly over his bare chest. "Jake?"

When he didn't answer, she sat on the other end of the couch and stared at the fire. After a moment Jake said quietly, "Don't push." Looking at her through the shadows, Jake rubbed the back of his neck and said, "I need to talk to you."

"Fine. What is it?" Morganna settled on one end of the couch, tucking her feet beneath her and covering them with the robe.

Jake studied her intently, his expression hard. "The whole countryside is gossiping. I should have known better than to take you on. Out here, a man doesn't have a female ranch hand. Much less one like you. They think I'm...that we're involved. Add that to Else's plans and you've got a mess. She expects us to turn up in Jasmine next Saturday night. It's a local dinner and dance. The family will want to meet you since it's apparent that you're my—"

"What would give them that idea?" Morganna interrupted curiously, and Jake shot her a hard look.

"You might as well know now. I haven't been around a woman since my wife died...haven't wanted to. My family—the Blaylocks—have been tossing women at me for years."

"Poor baby," Morganna cooed, instantly miffed at all the other women who'd been offered Jake on a platter.

"You've got a sassy mouth, lady. This isn't funny, unless you like qualifying as my mistress," Jake shot back. "You're living with me, and the gossips assume that we're sharing more than the roof."

Morganna smiled sweetly. "I've never been afraid of gossip. It usually runs its course."

"Not in Jasmine," Jake said darkly. "Not in this instance."

"Jake, are you protecting me?" she asked and read the evidence in his grim expression. Though Jake was misguided, she appreciated his sweet concern. "As chief executive officer of Larrimore Corporation, I'm exposed to gossip every day. I can handle it."

"Uh-huh," he agreed without commitment, then he moved toward her, lifting her and sitting with her on his lap. "Let's see just what you can handle."

"Now, Jake—" Morganna inhaled softly and wondered wildly when any man had ever held her on his lap, one of his hands spreading across her hip and the other flat against her

stomach. Those long fingers smoothed and caressed as Jake
lowered his lips to hers, his eyes slowly closing.

"Sweet," he murmured huskily, nibbling around her
parted mouth, then tasting her with the tip of his tongue.
While Morganna floated with his tender kisses, Jake gently
lowered her back to the couch. His hands stroked her,
smoothing the robe away while he pressed a trail of kisses to
her throat, nibbling at her lobe.

When his mouth touched her breast, she jerked against
the sweet sensation, cords running down her legs and heating her body. She gasped, shivering with the new emotion
rocketing through her. She lifted to him, holding her breath
while he gently tugged the tip of her breast. "Oh, my," she
whispered, her fingertips clinging to his bare shoulders,
stroking the sleek warmth.

Kissing his way to her other breast, Jake treated it equally,
his skin hot against her softness. "Blossom," he murmured, his teeth gently scoring the tips of her breasts to send
her quivering, melting and soaring into a golden shimmering cloud.

He trembled in her arms, his body heating hers while his
hands caressed and stroked, taking her higher. "You taste
sweet, Blossom," he whispered unevenly, his hand stroking
her leg from thigh to the arch of her foot. "Sweet..."

Soaring through emotions she had never experienced,
Morganna lifted her hips slightly, and Jake groaned shakily, his big hands warm and trembling as he gently cupped
her femininity, holding her possessively. Lying slightly over
her, his chest meeting the tips of her breasts, Jake shuddered, breathing unevenly, his fingers lightly caressing the
softness beneath her briefs. "You smell so good..." he
whispered roughly against her cheek, his face hot and rough.
"That sweet, woman scent—"

Then he was thrusting away from her, sitting upright, his
hair catching the firelight in blue lights as it swirled around
his face. "I've been without a woman's body for ten years,
Blossom," he whispered, his fingers pressuring her thigh as
though he didn't want to release her just yet. "Look. We're

different people. I don't need you messing in my life, and this isn't the way that it should happen for you—''

In the next instant Jake was gone, the fire surging with the draft from the door he had jerked open then closed silently.

Morganna lay trembling, unable to stop the tears that had been lurking around her all day.

Jake decided to let Morganna sleep the next morning. Her bed had creaked all night, and twice something that sounded like a boot had hit her door, bouncing to the floor. From the other side of the wall she had talked restlessly in her sleep. Before dawn Jake had carried his boots outside and jerked them on while he leaned against the house. Petey's smirk from the safety of the barn wasn't a pleasant thing to see. Jake would have preferred Morganna's soft mouth and sleepy green eyes. At five in the morning he would have preferred her snuggling against him. He left Petey to discover Morganna's morning mood and retreated to plow a field for planting hay.

Petey had smirked through Jake's instructions about the placing of the shingles that would arrive from the lumberyard. The smirk continued through Jake's instructions to signal if trouble occurred. The signal, one used for years, was a simple matter of lifting a white flag from the roof of the barn.

Swinging the tractor around in the field and aligning the plow tines to his last sweep, Jake shot a wary glance at his house.

Reaching the opposite end of the field, Jake wheeled the tractor around and set the tines again. He was licking his wounds because a business dynamo was throwing herself into ranch work. The deception he had begun nettled him. Nathaniel's resources had better pin the man who threatened Morganna and quickly. Jake didn't want to think about her reaction when she discovered why he had gone up that mountain in the first place. She would see her father and therefore, himself as certified chauvinistic, protective, club-bearing males, who had intervened...no, he corrected...who had challenged her capability to fend for herself.

Fending for herself and her brother, Paul, was a top priority. On her two telephone calls to her father, Morganna had denounced him for threatening and abusing Paul. With that dangerous little curve of her lips and with a soft clear voice, Morganna had told Larrimore how she could "demolish Larrimore Corporation with a few well-placed calls to stockholders." Nathaniel received precise instructions to package Paul and send him to her for protection. Paul was a sensitive soul, it seemed, damaged by Larrimore's high standards for manhood...outmoded standards, according to Morganna. If Paul was damaged when she returned, Morganna "would consider it open warfare and she couldn't be responsible for the outcome. Or Larrimore's profit loss." Then she had lifted her lips in that tight, little smile. Nathaniel's angry roar had swept across the room.

Deer ran along the fence of the plowed field, then leapt gracefully into the air. They landed on the other side, zigzagging into the pines. Jake discovered he had been grinding his teeth, and his jaw ached from tension, an emotion that didn't exist before Morganna—or at least, not to this extent. If Paul didn't measure up to Nathaniel's standards, he just might not have Morganna's tough will to survive. He could complicate the protection of the woman Jake considered rightfully his...at least for the duration. Then there were all the potential baby makers of the world waiting for Morganna....

Her infamous "husband list" and its fuzzy qualifications irritated him. Jake snorted. "Just a shade below USDA choice, I'd say."

His gloved hands tightened on the tractor's steering wheel, and he ground the gears on the tractor, startled by his dark mood.

His mood lasted until Petey's bowed legs shuffled over the top of the small knoll separating Jake from a view of the house. Waving his battered hat, Petey panted for breath while Jake leapt from the tractor and ran toward him. Jake's heart pounded, filling with terror. If that madman had Morganna—

"Boss. The shingles...they came...and..." Petey wheezed, swallowed and continued. "She's up there on the roof...hammering away...just hauled a ladder against the house and began carrying them up there. Wouldn't wait for you.... She used the signal flag to dust the barn."

While Petey gasped for breath, Jake's long legs were already carrying him toward the house. After a long look at the roof, he rammed his fingers through his hair and closed his eyes. The image of new shingles, nailed haphazardly across the old ones remained behind his lids. Then, in a flash, images of the two prime heifers he had sold to pay for the shingles appeared and smirked. Morganna's hammer banged away; nails rolled down the roof and plopped steadily at his boots.

"Hi, Jake," Morganna called, lifting her hammer in a wave. "There's nothing to this roofing business. Go on back to plowing or whatever. I should have this finished by suppertime."

Curds meowed and twined languidly around Jake's legs, showing off her new lean body. Jake glanced at the rounded feminine bottom wriggling up on the roof, providing him with an excellent view. He didn't realize he'd backed up, studying those two round shapes beneath her tight jeans, until he almost stepped on Curds. A roofing nail rolled slowly down the abused roof to plunk at his toe. "I need to make a phone call," he returned through his teeth.

Nathaniel answered his private line moments later, "Larrimore."

"What's the status on that maniac?" Jake demanded without pleasantries.

"We're still working on it," Nathaniel answered after a slight hesitation. "Is there a problem? Rita, my daughter's assistant, says she's having no trouble buffering my daughter's calls. Ah...Rita. There's a woman for you...soft, controllable, trustworthy...which brings me to a female who isn't. How is my daughter, Jake? Is she having a good time?"

"'A good time,'" Jake repeated flatly as nails continued to rain from the roof, making loud rolling sounds. "We need to talk, Nathaniel. Set it up...I'll check back."

"Uh...Jake, my daughter is rather cute in her own way, isn't she? Anything happening there...uh, you know, the old sparks flying between you?" Nathaniel probed.

"'Cute,'" Jake repeated flatly.

"Morganna is all right, isn't she?" There was a sharp crack to Larrimore's voice as though he would tear heaven and hell apart to keep his little girl safe.

"Your daughter is destroying my ranch, Nathaniel, and I'm feeling guilty as hell about keeping her here. Set up that meeting. I'll want a status report of exactly where your people are in the investigation," Jake ordered curtly. The sound of a ladder, sliding, then thudding to the ground, froze his hand in midair as he returned the telephone to the cradle.

Outside Morganna clung by her fingertips to the metal rain gutter, which was slowly bending to deposit her feet on the ground. She released the rain gutter and it hung there, vibrating with its last effort, bent at an odd angle and freed from its moorings. She glanced at Jake. "That can be easily fixed," she said, dusting her gloves together. "I'll do it in a minute."

While Jake hovered between kissing her, because she was safe, and doing something he'd probably regret immediately. Morganna spotted Curds and let out a soft wail of delight. "Oh, Jake! Curds must have had her kittens. Look how thin she is."

He took one last look at the patchwork roof, the fallen ladder, and the battered rain gutter, closed his eyes and followed Morganna—who was following Curds—into the barn.

Morganna's softly rounded derriere quivered slightly as she hopped over a scattered bundle of shingles and Jake's body reacted immediately. He grimly wondered about the permanent damages of frustrated passion to his hardened body just as Morganna dipped under a railing and knelt by Curds, who was proudly nursing her kittens.

"Oh, Jake, aren't they beautiful?" Morganna asked huskily, stroking one hungry kitten with her fingertip. "Aren't they?" she prompted, her green eyes glowing and her mouth softly curved as she looked up at him expectantly. Jake realized then that his heart had started beating again. He sat on his heels, watching her, fascinated by the way she stroked each kitten counting them. "Six. Six beautiful, precious kittens. Two grays, one gray with white boots, and oh, Jake, look . . . two all black with white boots and one calico. Aren't they pretty?"

With her hair gleaming in the shadows and her face glowing with excitement, Morganna stirred emotions Jake could not control. Leaning closer, Jake touched the calico kitten with his leather glove.

Then Morganna was watching him intently, her eyes dark and mysterious.

Time went swirling by, drifting minutes away like bits of gold dust caught on a sunbeam. Morganna's hand lay on his cheek, stroking it, finding the bones beneath his skin, tracing them as if seeing him for the first time.

Jake's heart stopped as she knelt between his thighs, her hands touching, fluttering along the lines of his jaw, his eyebrows . . . brushing as lightly as butterfly wings, warming like silk and sun, enchanting him in a tender web. Beneath her lashes, dark green eyes followed her exploring fingertips and Jake's chest ached. He inhaled sharply, startlingly aware of his body needing air, of needing Morganna like he needed air, he corrected as she leaned closer, studying his mouth.

Her lids drifted shut, her mouth pressing on his. First with a curious light drift of her lips across his and back again. Then lifting her mouth slightly, she tasted his upper lip, slowly, tentatively.

When her lips enclosed his bottom lip gently, Jake realized his gloved hands circled her waist. Her lips drifted to the side of his mouth, then the other, pressing a light kiss to warm and tease. She tilted her head slightly, lightly testing the fit and the slant of their lips. Her fingers flowed along his throat, his shoulders. Beneath her touch, Jake breathed quietly, fearing to move, savoring the sweet, tenuous bond.

One exploring finger swirled around his ear, sweeping away to linger in his hair. Those slender fingers caught him, opening to glide through his hair, to tighten gently at the back of his head, easing him nearer her mouth. Jake trembled, fighting the urge to draw her into his arms, letting her seek and taste and find him. Those floating hands brushed his shoulders, the fingers clenching. "Jake?" she whispered against his mouth, her green eyes looking deep, deep within his.

"Yes," he answered simply, falling into those eyes as his heart stopped beating.

Neither wanted to acknowledge Petey's first call. His second caught them unaware, and Morganna jumped to her feet suddenly, her face flushing.

The movement knocked Jake back into a soft cushion of hay where he lay winded. Morganna's soft "Oh, dear" was trapped by her fingers.

"Boss. You've got to stop resting in the middle of the day. You've got a call. Sounds like business." Petey's grin bounced off Jake to fasten on Morganna, whose bottom lip was trembling. Though Petey couldn't see, Jake enjoyed a tempting view of her sweater and the two thrusting points clearly visible to Morganna when she followed his gaze.

Jerking her eyes back to his, she shuddered and crossed her arms in front of her, the tilt of her chin daring him.

When she caught the thrust of his aroused body, Morganna's eyes widened and she swallowed. "I...ah...I think I'll just finish that roof now," she said huskily before walking out of the barn. Her unsteady weave at the door did wonders for Jake's ego, and he wondered absently if he'd slipped up a notch on the USDA grade A, prime-husband material list.

"Uh...boss. Telephone?" Petey prompted. Rising to his feet, Jake glanced at Petey's face. He looked again, startled by the wistful, dreamy expression of "Ain't love grand?" settling over the leathery wrinkles.

Nathaniel's deep barroom rasp wasn't the sound Jake wanted to hear in the next few minutes. He would have preferred Morganna's sweet, curious purrs peppered with a few cries of that surprised ecstasy. Jarred back into his arrangement with Morganna's father, Jake tasted the corrosive bitterness of guilt once more. "Admit it, Jake. My daughter is quite a woman under that business exterior. Sure, she can drive a guy nuts, but she's cute...well, not really that cute, when she's got the whole board of directors up in arms.... She's a regular little Joan of Arc over her brother, Paul. Damn. That boy's biggest ambition is to raise jumping frogs. That's fine for other people, but you know that 'fruit of my loins' stuff and hell...I just thought he'd step into my shoes."

"Set up a meeting and do it quick," Jake snapped, his gloved hand gripping the telephone. Above him, Morganna began hammering away, and the nails started rolling down the roof once more. Jake inhaled sharply. Part of him ached for release, part of him wanted to cuddle her, but the major portion of his emotions told him that at the moment he would enjoy wrapping his fingers around Nathaniel Larrimore's thick neck.

"You're single-minded today, Jake. Now...one last time. You have to admit that Morganna is cute...well...don't you think she's a little bit appealing as a woman?" Jake heard the last words as he replaced the receiver. All he had to do was wait through the hours until Larrimore appeared....

Then there was Morganna. Jake listened to another nail roll down the roof. "Cute," he repeated grimly, jerking on his gloves. For the moment, the highly creative CEO ruining his roof had to be stopped.

Jake slid into bed before dawn the next day, his body aching. Planting new fruit trees by moonlight hadn't

trimmed his desire for Morganna, nor the sound of her
sweet, surprised gasps as he kissed her breasts. However, the
physical effort was much better than listening to her muttering and the creaking springs throughout the night. Jake
slept lightly, awakening at each mutter, each creak. At first
light Petey arrived to prepare breakfast, glanced at Jake and
muttered something about "youth's hot blood stirring
around between dusk and dawn." When Jake shot him another black look, Petey cackled loudly, plopped on his hat
and announced, "Think I'll just keep out of the way for a
bit until the fur settles down."

For the next week Morganna slid Jake curious glances and
worked to raise the ranch's daily accidents. The vacuum
cleaner was an immediate fatality, sucking up her discarded
T-shirt. Morganna wound a spoon around the beaters of a
portable mixer and bleached Jake's jeans, creating huge
white spots in the denim. She discovered the iron and re-
garded it as a new invention, vowing to purchase one when
she returned home. Petey's leathery scowl deepened when
he found the scorched imprints of an iron on his clothing.
The men's white cotton underwear turned a mysterious
pink, and the kitchen sink clogged with the grease that
Morganna thought was hot water extracted from meat.

All the practical hand-me-down jeans Else had given
Morganna were tight and Jake found himself staring at her
rounded, swaying backside more than once. The sight of her
padding into the bathroom at midnight wearing his T-shirt,
loose boxer shorts and work socks bunched around her ankles destroyed his sleep. Then there was the time he came
into the house in the mid-afternoon, believing Morganna to
be cleaning out the chicken house with Petey, and discovered her sound asleep in the bathtub.

Unable to leave, Jake crouched beside the tub and
watched Morganna's fingers and toes move as she slept.
Awake, Morganna was in constant motion, and asleep her
body kept moving as though resenting the rest period. He
plucked a straw from her hair and fought looking at the pale
curves shimmering beneath the sudsy water. When he did

look, his body reacted immediately and Jake stood slowly, wiping his hand across the perspiration on his upper lip. Taking care, he stepped outside the bathroom, closed the door and slapped his hand against it. "Hey, is anybody in there?"

Jake fought against chuckling, when Morganna yelped from beyond the door and splashed violently. "Go away!" she sputtered. "Jake, don't you dare come in!"

Later, between cackling laughter, Petey described how Morganna had plunged into the chicken house, slid and fell on her backside. She gamely got up, brushed her gloved hands and backside and began shoveling the combination of feathers, straw and gray matter into a wheelbarrow. When she discovered the nature of that gray matter, she had asked, "You mean chickens aren't housebroken?" Astounded at Petey's answer, she'd flown off to the house for her bath.

When Saturday night came, Jake wished he'd never heard of Nathaniel Larrimore or his daughter. Morganna had produced a basic sheath, black hose and flats from the wreckage of her gear. She'd tossed the muddied sheath into the washer and dried it, proud of her new skills to cope with stains.

The sheath shrank, tightly fitting her body and exposing a slender length of thigh though her arms were covered with the long sleeves. She insisted firmly that women wore outfits like hers every day. In the short skirt, Morganna's legs looked endless, and Jake avoided looking at them while they drove into town. He felt very possessive and protective of that body and tried not to think of how her pale breasts pushed against the bodice, rounding softly above it. They quivered slightly when the truck bounced across a rut, and Jake fought to keep his eyes on the road.

Jake's knuckles whitened as he gripped the steering wheel. The night loomed before him, filled with Jasmine males staring at Morganna's neatly curved body.

Six

When Jake opened Jasmine's community center door for Morganna at six o'clock that night, the friendly, loud murmur stopped. A second later the rhythmic tapping spoons and guitar stopped playing. When she began taking away her camouflage camping coat, Jake gently took it from her. Unused to gallantry, like being lifted into the truck's seat and out again, Morganna ignored his dark looks when Else swept her away from him. The conversations began softly then rose again to the gentle roar. Morganna surveyed the huge community room with long tables lined with chairs. Appetizing scents hovered in the room, and children played tag through the legs of men dressed in western clothing. Women fluttered around the tables and carried food from a huge kitchen.

She hadn't experienced anything like the community get-together, and she wanted to savor every festive nuance. Else introduced her to men and women who were enjoying themselves and casting humorous glances at Jake. Jake, standing with a group of equally tall, dark men who bore the same distinct coloring and facial features, periodically shot her one of those dark, threatening looks, which Morganna returned with a cheery smile. She was unafraid of Jake's silent threats, having refused her father's intimidation at an early age, then a raft of high-powered businessmen later. Clustering males usually resented Morganna's presence, and she toyed with the idea of penetrating the Blaylock male circle as she had tormented her father's associates. Pushing the thought away for possible later action, she surveyed the friendly gathering of people who had known each other for a lifetime.

She endured Jake's dark looks through Else's introductions to the massive Blaylock family and members of the community. The entire town seemed to dote on Jake, and matrons grabbed him for a quick hug. Dressed in a red cotton sweater, jeans that clung to his long legs, and his polished Sunday boots, Jake was wickedly handsome. Morganna's heart stopped beating when she saw him holding a chubby black-haired child tenderly against him. He returned a juicy kiss and grinned at the three-year-old girl in his arms, straightening her ruffled, red polka-dot skirt. A four-year-old boy began tugging at Jake's leg and slowly crawled his way upward to be cradled in the crook of Jake's other arm.

Jake stood in the middle of the men, conversing seriously while the two children observed the room from their high perch. All the Blaylock men, including Jake, handled the children with ease and cared for their needs, while the women prepared the long tables of wonderful Spanish and "plain, old country cooking."

Hannah Blaylock swept Morganna away from Else and introduced her to the other members of the family. James, Logan, Roman and Rio politely dipped their dark heads when they were introduced to her, and Morganna quickly noted how courtly the men treated the females in their midst. Hannah's husband, Dan, immediately tugged her close and rested his hand over the third addition to their family, nestled snugly in her body. Morganna's heart lurched at the tender love passing between them, when Hannah, her long, russet hair contrasting with her husband's black hair, kissed him back.

The open expression of love startled Morganna for an instant, her heart aching. Expressing love and tenderness was not a Larrimore trait, and her father considered it a waste of time—unless he was pursuing a business deal or a new woman, in that order. Paul and she had grown closer, clinging to each other in the vast, wealthy loneliness. Hannah turned to her, paused and slipped her arm through Morganna's. "I grew up here, but I've never gotten over how beautiful this family is and the rich, close community feeling. You'll see. How is Jake adjusting to a woman living on his ranch?"

Morganna shot him a look and found him staring at her, his expression concealing this thoughts. "He's not an easy man to know," she answered truthfully. Suddenly she mourned for the moment when he'd drawn away from her that night.

"Are you an easy woman?" Hannah probed softly.

"Oh, we're not involved," Morganna stated quickly, mentally tucking her potential husband and baby maker lists away. "I'm just helping at the ranch this month. He needed an extra hand and I had the time. It's fascinating really. I've never had a chance to explore life on a ranch—"

"Uh-huh. Sure. Do you have any idea how many women have chased that man? Jake is known as that 'handsome as sin widower'. Else's been matchmaking for years, but Jake has frozen his heart since his wife died. He reminded me of an aloof, badly wounded wolf who was afraid to mate again. That happens, you know, some people never recover and I feared that he might be lonely forever. From the way he's looking at you, there's something in the air," Hannah whispered and grinned. "Dan used to look at me that same, passionate way." Her eyes shimmered with tears and she smiled tenderly. "He still does. How I love that man, though at first we had a rough time understanding each other."

Morganna inhaled, then caught Jake's hot dark eyes locked to her bosom. "I'm not Jake's...friend. He isn't my type and I'm certain that he has other interests." She hated the women who had experienced Jake, and she wondered how many he had pleased on his firelit couch and those sweet, searchingly hungry kisses. She rubbed the small place on her throat where his beard had scraped, remembering the uneven heat of his breath sweeping across her throat, her breasts. Then there was that possessive caress across her femininity, the gentle tightening of his fingers as though he was claiming her for his— Morganna shielded her blush and wondered if she were coming down with the flu.

Where Jake was involved, she plunged immediately into a sudden flush or a blank-minded tizzy. Like when he emerged from the bathroom earlier that night, his chest bare and gleaming with droplets of water. Unable to unlock her stare from that bronzed width, she had tripped over a rug, and Petey, trying to keep his casserole for the event from burning her, had backed into the open refrigerator. Dishes, bottles and last night's roast had spilled to the floor before Petey pivoted neatly and placed the hot casserole on a pad. "I'm gettin' used to her, boss," he had crowed, doing a little jig and slapping the pot holders along his thighs.

Morganna had no idea what Petey was getting used to. Her eyes locked with Jake's dark ones. He was burning her, consuming her, emotions swirling between them that she didn't understand. She had jerked her gaze away and focused on her fingers, which were gripping the countertop.

In that instant the fiery passion binding them was so strong she had almost stepped toward him. In Jake's taut face she had seen savage possession, tenderness and aching desire; her emotions had ignited brazenly. Morganna resented the loss of her control. A man like Jake was too dangerous to the life she wanted. Boxing him into a smoothly orchestrated, corporate marriage of convenience would be impossible.

Hannah's eyebrows lifted. "Morganna. You may not know this, but Jake hasn't looked—I mean even glanced at another woman since Dianne and their baby died in that wreck. The way he's looking at you now—as though he'd like to carry you off and make love to you. Take my advice...see Rio?" She nodded toward a younger Blaylock brother. "He's unmarried, though we're looking for a suitable girl for him. If he asks you to dance later, do it. I'll bet Jake will be there in half a second."

"I'm not that kind of woman—" Morganna hesitated when Hannah looked at her curiously. "I mean men have never really been interested in me—as a woman."

Hannah's laughter rippled delicately. "From the looks Jake is giving you, he isn't thinking of your business skills. That dress is a man-killer. I've always suspected that Jake was a very passionate man, though he glosses over those fierce emotions with his charm."

Morganna stared blankly at Jake and found his gaze running down her slowly, hungrily. The impact of that stare pushed the breath from her. "Oh, my."

"Yes." Hannah laughed again and placed her palm over the baby shifting in her womb. "Oh, my."

Throughout the preparations for the dinner, Morganna noted that the Blaylock men carefully attended the women's directions when asked to fetch or carry. During the traditional Blaylock powwow, a male-only tradition of the family that dated back to their Apache days, the men stood when a woman neared them and politely nodded. Hannah winked and Morganna followed her into the midst of the powwow to ask Dan a simple question. While Hannah's five-foot-nine height blended well in the predominantly tall family, Morganna's neck began to ache from constantly looking upward. "I do that once in a while, just to test the waters," Hannah explained after they left the circle. "Keeps them on their toes."

Someone plopped a black-haired infant in Morganna's arms, and she stared helplessly at the squirming bundle swathed in a pink shawl. Then the baby began to cry softly. Morganna had never held a baby in her arms, had expertly avoided holding them. The baby cried louder, and instinctively Morganna cuddled the infant closer, rocking it against her until the baby nestled and sighed against her. Fascinated by the tiny sucking motions of the baby's soft mouth, Morganna rocked her gently and bent to nuzzle the fat silky cheek.

She glanced up and found the everyone in the room was watching her. The look in Jake's eyes as he crossed the room to her caused her heart to race. She had an image of people smiling, gently nudging one another and nodding, then Jake towered over her, his finger secured by the baby's tiny fist. Her throat dried while Jake continued to stare down at her, the tiny fist gently thudding his warm finger against her chest. "Ma'am, you are truly a sight," he whispered unevenly, then slowly bent his head to kiss her.

When he lifted his head, his eyes holding hers, there was one second of absolute silence in the crowded room. The next instant the Blaylock brothers gave out a loud shout. Jake pivoted away from her like a gunfighter protecting his backside. He quickly shielded his fierce, stunned expression while each brother caught his respective wife and bent her over his arm in a deep, romantic kiss. Rio, as the unwed brother, swept a passing girl into his arms and kissed her.

Jake cursed beneath his breath, as though just awakening to the rippling aftershocks of what he had caused. The Blaylock wives seemed dazed and flustered when released, and their husbands gently directed them to the long dinner tables. The girl Rio had kissed flopped limply into a nearby chair and stared into space for a full three minutes before she blushed.

Morganna was astonished with the Blaylock males' courtly manners. Each brother handled his wife as though she was something quite precious to him. "My," she whispered through sensitive lips, then noted that somehow Jake had taken the baby from her and cradled it in one long arm, while he held her hand with the other.

Jake frowned, his taut jaw moving. He eased the baby to a woman who grinned impishly at Morganna. Then Jake was drawing her to stand in line at a food-laden table, his hand riding her waist. There was an impatience simmering around him, as though he resented her. Taking the plate he handed her, Morganna jabbed her elbow into his flat stomach. She hadn't asked him to kiss her after all. "I thought you were worried about gossip, Jake. You've just started an entire century's worth of it . . . you had no business—" She pushed her lips into a smile, returning one of the children's curious stares. "You had no right to kiss me like that in front of everyone."

"No? It settled down the bachelors. I don't want a porch full of them in the morning. You're not dancing with Rio or anyone but me. Get that out of your head right now," he said stiffly, placing the flat of his hand low on her back and edging her to the huge sliced roast beef and ham.

"Stop herding me." Morganna jabbed her elbow into his stomach again and watched with satisfaction when he gave a soft grunt.

"Blossom, somebody needs to ride herd on you. Since I brought you, that responsibility falls to me." Using his body, Jake nudged Morganna toward the bowls of mashed potatoes and baked macaroni and cheese and scalloped potatoes. If he was irritated, it wasn't her fault, and he could take his dandy little temper someplace else.

"Huh. I wonder how I managed to survive without you, Jake."

Jake's hard mouth curved with amusement, and he nudged her forward a bit. She resisted the wall of his body, turning her shoulder into his broad chest to look up at him. "Mr. Tallman, if you please."

"You're holding up the line, ma'am," he said, nodding politely to Hannah, who had been watching with interest. When Hannah bent to tend the toddler at her side, Jake reached across Morganna to dip a hefty portion of corn casserole into his plate. His arm brushed her breast and when Morganna looked up at him sharply, she found Jake's expression grim, his eyes locked to her tight bodice. Tiny beads of perspiration dotted his upper lip, and Morganna shivered, suddenly very warm.

"You're pushing me, Jake." Morganna stopped talking. She forced her gaze to leave Jake's heated one, locking on the heaping platters of food. "These look delicious," she managed in a faltering husky voice. "You know I've never been to anything like this in my life. What are those tortillas things with the cheese and meat fillings?"

"Enchiladas. Several of the dishes are Tex-Mex, a blend of southwest and Mexican dishes. There's Idabelle's salsa—pure liquid fire." Jake's big hand caressed her waist, edging her slightly against him. The fierce edge of his possession confused Morganna, who was unused to any man claiming her as Jake was obviously doing.

Morganna tried not to think of the fire Jake's body ignited within her own and studied the dishes intently. "I can cook this. Let's stop at the local supermarket before going home."

"Home," Jake repeated, bending down to nuzzle her temple. "I like the sound of that right now." The achingly tender sound in his deep voice curled around her.

"But we just got here...." The heated look in Jake's eyes dried her throat and she looked away, shielding her flush.

For the next hour Morganna experienced her first small-town social, and whenever she turned Jake loomed at her side. Often his rough hand would wrap around hers, his thumb caressing her skin. The sensation of being cuddled was new, uncomfortable to Morganna, who had survived a lifetime without it. She couldn't remember a time when a man had stood by her and rested his hand on her waist. The possessive gesture unnerved Morganna who couldn't stop drumming her fingers. She thought about returning tit for tat and looping her arm around his waist. The mental picture stunned her; she had never been cuddled, nor cuddled in return.

Hannah stood next to Morganna while the men removed the tables and placed the chairs against the walls to form a dance floor. Morganna returned Jake's dark look, and Hannah laughed aloud. "It's a territorial thing—a man staking out the woman he wants. Jake is making certain that every man here knows you're his. Rather an antiquated, possessive attitude, but very romantic when he hasn't seemed to notice all those begging women for years. Passed them by politely, because he knew that Else's wooden spoon would be waiting for him if he didn't. He can be devilishly charming and sidestep a woman at the same time.''

Lowering her voice, Hannah continued, ''For a time after the accident, Jake's refrigerator was loaded with dishes from single women. Lettie Marshall actually put a sedative in her cookies so that she could get into his bed and oblige Jake to marry her. Petey threw the cookies to the chickens and they slept through an entire day. Judith Hensicker ruined a perfectly good tire to have him change it and Fanny Olingberg reportedly once installed herself in his bed one winter night. When Jake found her, he called Petey to take her home. When Fanny turned up the next night, Jake slept at our place. Else teased him ruthlessly about filling that vacancy against squatters.''

Morganna asked the question that had been troubling her. ''Tell me about Jake's wife?''

''Dianne? A childhood sweetheart...sweet. Just the balm Jake needed to soothe away his rough younger years. They never argued...it was an easy, loving relationship. They waited years for that baby. When Dianne and his son died, we worried about him. Two long years passed before Jake began to paste his life together. With you here tonight, he is different person. Sort of cute to see him dance around a woman for once. I never suspected Jake to be a cuddler, but he definitely likes touching you. Serves him right for being the county heart breaker, and starving all those hungry women.''

''This whole body play thing is interesting,'' Morganna returned. ''I've never really noticed how often men touch women. This family seems to have interesting characteristics. I'm certain that Jake is just acting as he's been taught. I'm merely the object of his training at the moment...since he is forced to act as a semi-host for me at this dinner.''

Hannah ran her hand over the area of her pelvis which encased her unborn baby. "Jake is a tender man. Blaylock men respect motherhood, revere it. They make wonderful fathers, if a little too protective."

Morganna remembered Jake's expression when she held the baby, her heart turning flip-flops as she found him in the crowd. Tall, wickedly handsome with longish hair and dark skin, Jake tossed a giggling toddler into the air. He caught the chubby girl neatly and began to sway as though dancing. The girl's tiny hands pressed against his dark cheeks and she kissed him with a bob of her curly head. His easy grin, a flash of white teeth in a tanned, ruggedly handsome face, dried Morganna's throat.

"Well, that's his first real smile in years.... That man is one happy hombre. Funny, I've never thought of Jake as loveable. Charming, yes, but distant, as if he wanted to keep a portion of his life away from everyone, even from Dianne.... Right now he's downright cute. We've waited a long time to see him like this," Hannah stated softly. "Unless I'm picking up the wrong signals, he's in the mood for— dancing. That or another territorial Blaylock thing, parking with his girl by the old adobe building. According to an old Spanish legend, that old crumbled mess of adobe bricks is the best place to sort out the basics with the male at hand. Sort of a testing. You'd be perfectly safe with Jake, he's an absolute gentleman."

"I can't picture Jake doing that. But dancing? Oh, I hope he doesn't ask me. I don't know how," Morganna protested as a caller stepped in front of the four-member band and announced a "Waltz, then a Texas two-step." The crowd parted for the two tall men, Jake and Rio, walking toward her.

Rio, younger and smoothly handsome to Jake's rugged masculinity, dipped his head toward Morganna, his lips curving. Jake stepped past him, sweeping Morganna into his arms. "Not this time," he stated flatly, drawing her body against his and placing his hands on her waist.

She pushed against his stomach, panicking. "Jake. Stop. My agenda hasn't left time for dancing. I'll just watch until I get the hang of it. I learned how to run a board meeting like that—"

"Put your arms around my neck, Blossom," Jake murmured, smoothing her waist with his hands when the fiddler began to play. Jake led her in a slow, stately waltz, his eyes locking with hers. Morganna had a swirling image of people stepping back, of Hannah leaning against Dan, of Else beaming widely, her arm around her husband, Joe.

"Uncle Jake, you said *I* was your best girl, now you're dancing with *her!*" A childish voice complained and was shushed.

Two hours later Morganna huddled on the passenger side of the truck and glared at Jake, who had just lifted her easily and deposited her into the high seat. His romantic behavior had startled her, kept her reeling throughout the night. Freewheeling through her business challenges hadn't prepared her for Jake's singular attention.

Morganna frowned and remembered Hannah's description of Jake's extended bachelor state. There was something definitely predatory and wolfish about him when he looked at her—as though she were his favorite piece of luscious, warm cherry pie topped with a scoop of creamy ice cream. Morganna had fended off several hormonal cowboys in her time, but Jake didn't quite fit the mold. For one thing, he wasn't distracted by the number of attractive women laminating themselves to his tall, lean body. His interest in her was very focused, very unnerving.

The mystery deepened. There was simply no reason for Jake to romance her unless he had a private bet. Though Freddie Mills and his college chums may have pursued her for the sport, Jake wasn't the sort. She couldn't risk the devastation of his playacting, and wondered how hard he had to work to pretend his arousal that night on the couch. Or at the buffet line, when he had stood behind her with his hand resting on her shoulder, his body touching her back.

The image of the infamous Fanny Olingberg's well-proportioned body and frothy blond hair lurked too near. There had to be ulterior motives for Jake's attentions, when he was known to be a man who avoided female liaisons. There had to be a reason for the way his large hand had repeatedly curled around the nape of Morganna's neck, his thumb caressing that sensitive cord by her ear. Each time he did it, she shivered, and Jake grinned, stunning her mindless for a full heartbeat. She could return the favor, but then her repertoire of touching men's bodies in susceptible places was limited. The thought enraged her. When Jake crossed in front of the truck to the driver's side, she decided the best method of discovering motivations was to attack. When he opened his door, she said, "You deliberately set out to humiliate me. You antagonized and embarrassed me."

Jake paused, slammed his door shut and looked blankly across the shadows at her. "What?"

She slashed out her hand in a sweeping gesture. "All this attention, the way you wouldn't let anyone dance with me, the way you pulled me on your lap in front of everyone. I am a—"

"Top-notch CEO, an assertive businesswoman," he finished dryly and started the truck. Placing it in gear and shifting, Jake set a steady pace toward an isolated knoll overlooking Jasmine. The moon outlined a huge lonely pine in the center of the knoll; a crumbling adobe brick building sat apart, moonlight shooting through the windows. Jake parked the pickup in the dark and turned off the motor. His arm stretched across the back of the seat to her, and his thumb stroked the side of her throat. "Tell me, Ms. CEO, ma'am. Have you ever watched submarine races in Colorado?"

Seven

"Submarines? Where?" Morganna sat up, scanning the moonlit field. In the next second she was scooped onto Jake's lap. She resisted momentarily, then decided not to give him that victory and remained still. The legendary Blaylock bachelor legend couldn't be involved. Not with her. "That was sneaky. Why are you acting like this?"

His lips curved in a smile, along her throat and those fabulously long lashes tickled her skin. Morganna noted distantly that all Blaylocks had striking eyes and lashes and that the babies were adorable. "If we go home now, Blossom, I'll be in your bed the first time it creaks," he whispered, nuzzling her throat. "This small space is perfect to taste you the way I've been wanting to all night, without allowing more."

"Oh," she whispered weakly, while Jake continued nibbling along her throat. When the tip of his tongue traced her ear, she shivered, staring straight at the cattle grazing in the moonlit pasture in front of them. Trying to be firm while her heart was fluttering beneath Jake's caressing hand was more difficult than keeping Larrimore's board of directors from each other's throats.

Unprepared for the heat sweeping over her, Morganna turned nervously to admonish Jake. Instead she met his lips, and between nibbling kisses, he cradled her against him and stripped her jacket away. "Finally," he whispered unevenly against her cheek. "This dress should be banned."

Unused to raising male temperatures or flushing wildly, Morganna found her fingertips fluttering along Jake's strong shoulders. She forced them to still. "I . . . it's just my basic sheath. I always carry one for emergencies. I really should have packed my strand of pearls. My camouflage coat doesn't match at all."

She closed her lips, realizing belatedly that her unsteady emotions caused her to blather nervously.

Jake's hair was cool along her chest as he pressed kisses across the rounded tops of her breasts. Morganna's fingertips dug into his shoulders while her emotions fought the equatorial storm. She closed her eyes, trying to drag the shreds of her resistance together. "Now, Jake . . . I've been thinking." She tried to remember her thoughts, her fingers drumming against his taut shoulders. They stopped, lingered on the warm pads of muscle, then stroked him lightly.

"Mmm?" he murmured, lifting her slightly to nuzzle her breasts. "You have beautiful breasts, Blossom," he whispered unevenly as she found the sheath eased upward and away from her body, leaving her in a lacy black bra and pantyhose.

"Breasts?" Morganna blinked and forgot to breathe while she thought through the intimate compliment. Of course she had breasts, but no man had mentioned them in that soft, deep, rich, appreciative tone as if she were meant for him alone. No male had ever called her anything sweet and fragile. "Blossom?" she whispered as Jake eased the black strap of her bra down one pale shoulder, then the other. A moment later her bra hung from the mirror and Jake was kissing the tip of her left breast, lifting her slightly to draw her pantyhose off and tuck them in the glove box.

Her breasts ached intensely, the incredibly sweet need for Jake's warmth pushed deep within her. Startled by the awakening of her body, by its sudden fierce desires, Morganna shivered. Jake's eyes flicked down her body, his dark hand sweeping over her in a light, trembling caress.

She leaned back, lifting her breasts to his seeking mouth, straining against the tiny constrictions within her lower body. "Blossom... because you're sweet as a flower and so perfect," he answered huskily, stroking his warm, rough hand lightly down her body, then sweeping his fingers gently upward until they curved gently over her soft femininity.

"Jake..." Morganna murmured helplessly as those long, skillful fingers moved slightly, just within her. Holding on to the back of the seat, Morganna shivered, reeling with the passion flowing through her. She wanted his heat against her, his clothing swept away.

"Blossom," he whispered roughly, urgently. Then she discovered that she'd ripped his buttons from his shirt, her hands roaming the crisp hair covering his chest.

In the moonlight Morganna watched her fingers glide over his skin, flowing across his rough jaw to touch his lips. He sucked her fingers, one by one, his eyes flickering beneath the shadowy length of his lashes. She leaned against him, nuzzling his throat as he had hers and pressing bits of kisses across his hot cheek to his ear. Jake shifted suddenly, his arms holding her tighter.

The heavy, rapid pounding of his heart against her breast fascinated Morganna. She had never experimented with seduction, and Jake's response to her attempts sent her ego flying. When the tip of her tongue circled his ear, Jake inhaled sharply, his fingers pressing gently, finding her intimately. "Blossom...." She loved the ache in his deep voice, the urgent power of his body lifting beneath hers as his clothing slid away.

"Jake," she whispered against the heavily beating pulse in his throat and squirmed against him, uncomfortable with the unfulfilled aching in her body.

He shuddered, his desire pushing intimately between her legs. "Oh, no," he muttered almost helplessly. She squirmed a little, adjusting to the hard length just entering her. Testing the situation and feeling as if she was on a golden plateau of heady desire, she tentatively pushed down and Jake's arms tightened around her, his breath coming in short, hot strokes along her throat. "This isn't what I wanted—"

"I've never been an underachiever, Jake," she whispered when he finished kissing her. She wanted him desperately, her body incomplete and yearning.

"Blossom . . ." he returned in a rough whisper, his palms caressing her breasts, stroking them as she moved against him. "This isn't the place . . . or what I had in mind."

She trembled, aching for more than the tip of him. "I've made love in a car before," she assured him, to protect his sense of honor. Jake's honor was a serious thing she decided immediately. She couldn't allow him to feel as though he had taken advantage of her.

He kissed her tenderly, his eyes gentle in the shadows. "Really?"

"Well . . . it wasn't much. A hurried affair actually," she whispered, needing to be honest with him and shivering with her need to become one with this incredibly gentle, tender warrior. She closed her eyes, pushing her hips slightly against him as she fought the rippling constrictions deep in her body. "It didn't feel like this," she managed when she could whisper. She looked at him helplessly, "Oh, Jake, help me. . . ."

His mouth was tender, gently destroying her fears, parting and teasing her with his tongue in rhythmic movements. Gently, easily lifting, Jake entered her.

There was a sharp rasp of pain, and she gasped, fighting the swirling emotions within her. The beauty of their joined bodies held her still, her eyes meeting his as he lay there, letting her absorb all the power lodged fully, deep within her. His thumb brushed away a tear, and she realized slowly that she had been crying. "Blossom," Jake whispered huskily, smoothing her with his gentle hands.

Morganna concentrated on the wonder of their bodies, the startling constrictions taking her. She braced her hands against his shoulders as he slid deeper. "I really didn't think this would work," she whispered between gasps.

"Such a romantic," he whispered unevenly, his large hand stroking her back slowly, sensuously.

She cleared her throat, holding him tightly. The unique physical bonding enchanted her, the magic pulsating through her veins, heating her. "I'm a businesswoman, after all. There is the matter of logistics. But it is working, isn't it?"

Remaining still, Jake smiled tenderly in the shadows. "It hasn't just yet, sweetheart. But if you don't stop squirming like that, testing me, we might find out too quickly for your first time. Could you lie still for a minute?"

"Oh, Jake, this is so exciting," she returned shakily, lying fully on him, ready to sink into whatever pleasure he offered.

His body tensed beneath her and Jake muttered a curse, startling her as he very carefully eased her up and away from him. "You're getting dressed now," he ordered, sweeping her dress back over her and jamming on his jeans. "Something is moving out there."

Jake's soft grunt followed his long legs easing over the floorboard shift. He cursed beneath his breath, something about not being a half-grown, hot-pants teenager anymore. His hand pressed low on her stomach, his long fingers pushing into the material covering the juncture of her thighs. He cupped her firmly, gently as if arguing fiercely with his needs. "I'm sorry for this."

Shivering with reaction, the incomplete ache burning within her, Morganna realized that her hand was locked to Jake's hard thigh. She was fiercely possessive of the heavy muscle sliding beneath her palm, reluctant to release him. Then his fingers slid through hers, his palm large and safe against hers. She liked that blending of his dark skin with hers, the uniquely tender and sweetly old-fashioned bond...though currently she would have preferred another bond, her body cold without his. She glanced up at him and squirmed uncomfortably. While Jake had filled her completely, something seemed to be lacking in the overall event. . . .

"Look over there." He nodded toward a moonlit field. An old truck without headlights glided along a small herd of calves. "That's Tyree Lang. He hangs out with a bunch of teenage boys—school dropouts—who step into trouble at every turn. Before the Blaylocks reclaimed me, I was just like them. Right now it looks like he's rustling The Clover Leaf spread's prime Angus calves. They'll bring a good market price for veal."

"What do you suggest we do?" Morganna shivered, remembering the four tiny bottle-feeding calves and their lovely chocolate-colored eyes in Jake's barn. She vowed silently never again to eat her favorite veal parmesan.

"We?" he returned flatly, easing the truck into neutral gear so that it began to coast down the knoll. "We're going to keep on his blind side until we're closer. Those boys need mechanical training and tools, but they've rigged that old motor to outrun most race cars. This would be the first time I've been near when Tyree pulled anything, and I want to catch him red-handed."

"Oh." Morganna glanced at Jake's hard frown. "You won't hurt him, will you?"

He shot her a sharp look. "I intend to make this time count, Morganna. Scare him bad enough that he'll think twice before trying it again. When I open the door, you slide under the wheel and hold it steady along his passenger side. He's about to find himself with an unexpected guest."

"Me? Drive this?" She scanned the huge steering wheel.

Jake shot her another quick, appraising glance. "Don't tell me. You can't drive."

The large dashboard loomed in front of her, and not a push button in sight. She remembered her awful experience with her father's low-slung, super sports car and the horrible way he received news of his deceased clutch. Cars shouldn't be made with two pedals so much alike, and her left foot resisted coordination with her right side. "Of course, I can drive...I took lessons when I was twenty-two...but nothing this big or elaborate—"

"It's a standard shift, an H pattern." Jake started the motor, pressing his bare foot against the gas petal, shifted and eased closer to Tyree's. "It's in neutral. All you have to do is steer. When I jump, steer away from Tyree and shift into gear, or just turn off the ignition key...."

He opened the door, standing alongside Tyree's truck for a moment, then leaping into the darkness. Morganna gripped the huge wheel with both hands, fighting the hard tug and searching for the ignition key. The steering wheel fought her hands and the truck careened toward the only tree in the entire moonlit pasture. Adjusted for Jake's length, the seat was too far back. She sat on the edge of the seat to make up the distance while the truck bumped over a rock, sideswiped the tree and stopped just feet away from an innocent little black calf.

Morganna sat in the cab, her hands gripping the wheel, while the other vehicle squealed to a stop a distance away. A youth's voice, uncertain and angry, yelled and a door opened on the driver's side only to be slammed shut. The calves bawled and milled in the pasture. Morganna prayed they wouldn't attack her en masse. She remembered vivid flashes of movie stampedes and clung to the wheel until her hands ached, slick with sweat. Tyree's truck sat in the moonlight while her heart raced, and she fought the nausea of fear gone past. Then slowly the boy's truck began to turn and drive toward her, the headlights bouncing with each bump. When it stopped, Jake got out, walked to the driver's side, bent and spoke quietly. He straightened, stood in the moonlight and watched the truck circle the calves and begin herding them back.

Sliding to the passenger side of the bench seat, Morganna watched as Jake walked around his truck, paused at the back bumper and walked to the cab. In a lithe movement, he was inside and starting the engine, his expression grim as he drove home. "Pretty difficult to dent a fender in the middle of a twenty-acre pasture with one tree,'' he said tersely as the fender rattled behind them with every bump.

''I can't be held responsible,'' she sniffed, crossing her arms over her chest. ''Something is wrong with the steering. It won't move.''

''Uh-huh,'' he returned without commitment, following the path of the other truck. He grimaced briefly when the fender rattled.

Distracting Jake at this point wouldn't be easy, but she tried. ''Cattle rustling. That's a serious offense, isn't it?'' she asked as Jake's frown deepened.

''Bad enough. Worse than the petty stuff he's been into. He's smart, learns quick. But he's not cut out for this country. A vocation technical school would make a big difference in his life. He's got to get his high school degree. Maybe college. I'd send him and others if I could.''

Parking in front of the house, Jake shot Morganna another scowl in the shadowy cab. ''Tyree will be around tomorrow afternoon to talk.... You sit still, ma'am, until I come around to collect you,'' he ordered. His low, deadly tone caused Morganna to slide her fingers away from the door handle. Then Jake was lifting her easily, carrying her into the house.

While Morganna's body ached, feeling strangely empty and cold, Jake's was wonderfully warm and hard. Attempting to soothe what appeared to be ruffled male feathers, she gently laid her head on his shoulder. She lacked experience in that gentler art, but Jake mattered enough to try. She wanted him in a better mood, thus laying the ground to continue the personal business that had been interrupted. She really, really hoped there was more to lovemaking than her first two experiences, though by comparison Jake's was much better. Instantly his arms tightened around her and she was pleased with her first effort in cuddling him. ''Morganna, you've been drumming those busy little fingers since we started home. You've had enough...uh... excitement for one night. At this point I think the best thing is for us to go to bed...separately.''

He eased her to stand on the floor. "You're not wearing a thing under that dress, are you?" he murmured, running a fingertip along the top of her bodice and warming her sensitive flesh. He looked so vulnerable, so wary, that Morganna wanted to try more cuddling exercises.

Placing her hand experimentally on the flat of his hard warm stomach, Morganna licked her dry lips and mentally circled the notion of pushing Jake to the floor and having her way with him. Her downward glance proved that his desire had not lessened, though Jake stepped back from her. "Don't push me, Blossom. You need space to think about this. For me tonight meant one thing, for you it could mean another. Right now my control is a notch off center."

Then suddenly he moved past her, the latch on his bedroom door clicking softly behind him.

Morganna stared at that closed door. She had learned that at times business could wait and at times one must forge forward before ground in communications was lost. Clearly this was one of those forging times, for she intended to experience Jake's tenderness again, this very night. Morganna had never hesitated when a prime property or stock needed her takeover and Jake was very prime, indeed. She considered his decision to leave her, and decided that she hadn't agreed for him to chairman their little board of directors. Her vote hadn't been counted and she lacked his gallantry.

Morganna stripped off her dress, took a fleeting shower, and because she was uncertain of the protocol or the proper clothing, she opted for the dress again. She operated on the theory that if something works, don't fix it. If Jake liked it a first time, he would like it a second time.

She jerked his door open and stepped into the pool of moonlight. Her simmering anger veered sharply when she saw him lying full length on the wide bed, his arms behind his head and his jeans unsnapped. She wondered if he would leave the house as he had when the curvaceous, delectable Ms. Olingberg had warmed his bed. "I think you better call it a night, Blossom," Jake said huskily, his voice raw. "You're too new to this. Give yourself time to think."

She shivered, needing his warmth. "I can't. My legs won't move," she whispered, leaning back against the door. "I'm where I want to be."

Jake rose slowly, a masculine length of power and grace, gliding through the shadows until he stopped just inches from her. Towering over her, Jake placed his hands flat on the door, his eyes searching her pale upturned face. "Yes," she whispered, a sound barely heard over her rapidly beating heart. "Yes, Jake."

Jake's black eyes searched her face slowly, his body warming hers. If he left her, she would shatter.... Then Jake's angular features softened, his mouth curving sensually. "Come here, sweetheart. Let me warm you...show you how it can be...."

Sweeping her up, Jake carried her to his bed. The old-fashioned gesture was sweet, and she would remember it forever. There were certain benefits in the way Jake treated her—as though she was extremely feminine and desirable. She closed her eyes, infusing the feeling, wrapping it tightly in her memories. No other man had reached that quivering, soft core she had protected her entire lifetime.

Standing her on her feet once more, Jake eased the dress away until she stood, pale and curved in the moonlight flooding the room from the window. His jeans slid to her discarded dress, and Jake framed her face with his work-rough hands. "This is how a man loves a woman, Blossom...."

The kiss was searching, devastatingly sweet, and when it ended, Morganna lay entangled with Jake's warm body, his mouth and tongue promising, urging.... When she trembled, Jake moved slowly to cover her body. He lifted slightly away and opened a foil package he'd taken from the nightstand.

Then gently, gently, he began to enter her, his tall body shuddering. She stroked the nape of his neck, soothing the taut cords there. Nuzzling the side of her throat, Jake caressed her breasts, running his hands down to her thighs, pressing ever deeper. Again she felt the slight rasp of pain, and he stilled, waiting. "Easy...give yourself time.... You're tight inside, Blossom. Your first time was with me in the truck, not years ago."

She blushed, smoothing his taut arms. "You mean all those years I thought that I—"

Then she heard Jake's first low chuckle. He shifted and she closed her eyes with the pleasure. "Honey, I'm your first."

Above her his strained features were tender and he shivered. "I've been doing all the touching, Blossom. A man likes to be touched, too." With that he took her hands, stroking them against his sides.

"I can't wait, Jake," she cried softly, her body flowing upward. She found that wonderful fullness, the ache, easing for a heartbeat. Then he moved, easing deeper and she cried out with pleasure.

Jake began to lift and fall slowly, tutoring her as he watched her amazed expression of delight. The cords on his arms strained as he bent to kiss her breasts, to suckle them. "Sweet...so sweet...come with me...."

The tiny contractions began to flow, harder, driving her on, and Jake breathed sharply, his body lowering to hers. Holding her tightly, he drove them both to the edge and Morganna gathered him closer. They were running faster, faster...seeking...then Jake cried out and the warm tide washed over Morganna, easing away the tremendous sweet tension that had been pushing her.

Jake's heart thudded wildly against her, his head sharing the pillow as his hands stroked her trembling body. "I should run your bath," he managed unevenly, cuddling her close.

She hugged him, unwilling to allow him to move away. Resting lightly against her, he was secure and warm. She could do with a century of cuddling, of tangling with Jake's long, hard body. "Jake, that was wonderful...."

His smile tickled the side of her throat, his kisses nibbling toward her ear. He flicked her lobe with the tip of his tongue, and once more those quivering sensations began to curl deep inside her. "Was it? I had plans for a longer engagement."

"Really? You mean there's more? This lasts longer?" she asked hopefully, enchanted by Jake's wide grin. Squirming closer, Morganna touched his nipple curiously and watched it contract. When he inhaled, she bent to taste that flat nub. The startling result thrust at her again and immediately her body responded, contracting around him. "Oh, Jake...oh, Jake...." Eager to learn, to find that rocketing pleasure, she slid over him and pushed her hips downward.

Taking care, Jake caressed her back, found her breast and teased it with his lips and tongue. Then Morganna was arching, seeking the ultimate pleasure and Jake sighed deeply, his palms settling on her pale buttocks. "Morganna...shh, love...shh," he whispered as her startled little gasps filled the room.

"Oh, dear...oh, dear, oh, dear, oh...oh..." When Jake turned to draw her beneath him, the bed creaked and they slid to the floor in a padding of blankets and clothing. "Oh!" she exclaimed in a soft gasp, one last time before collapsing on him.

She awoke a heartbeat or an aeon later, his hands soothing her flushed, limp body. "I could be quite skilled at this in no time at all...I can do this, Jake," she said, allowing the glow within her to escape in a smile.

"Yes, you can and you do it very well, sweetheart," he agreed very, very slowly. The rich contentment in his tone brought her head up, and Morganna indulged her busy fingers by tracing Jake's rugged face. He caught a fingertip in his lips, biting it gently, and she giggled, excited about the loving play.

"Oh, Jake, that was marvelous. I've never felt so...so torrid," she sighed, sitting up and studying him for the first time. A marvelous tall blend of muscle and dark skin, Jake's length sprawled out like a beautiful new territory waiting to be explored. She touched his navel, hidden in the shadowy line of hair sliding down from his chest, and Jake inhaled sharply as those busy fingers traced his body. "You are so beautiful," she whispered in awe.

"Let's try for that longer engagement," he whispered hoarsely.

A silky web of Morganna's fragrant hair slid across Jake's cheek and he kissed it before opening his eyes. Refusing to let him leave her, Morganna had held him closely all night, her soft arms and legs snaring him. Tangled with her, he breathed quietly and stroked her warm body beneath the quilt. Snuggled against him, she was soft and limp. Jake smiled and noted the way she cuddled against him, then was still. For a time at least, Morganna's agile, restless body lay heavily against him. It was a quiet time, allowing him to think about Morganna and how she had returned his love.

There was more to making love with her than easing their bodies, there was fulfillment and gentler emotions swirling around them. They had shared the night and his bed and something else far deeper.

Inhaling slowly, breathing their scents, Jake knew that he had given Morganna his essence, his life and his future. More than the fevered lovemaking, he wanted the ease he was experiencing now—the relaxed, tender completion of his soul. He was glad he had waited, and fate brought her to him when it was time.

He frowned at a small red patch on her pale shoulder and bent to rub his lips across it. Though he'd ridden his passions, controlling his strength and hunger, he'd hurt her.

He stroked the length of her back, and Morganna stretched against him luxuriously, like a cat being petted. Drawing the heavy quilt over her bare shoulder, Jake settled down quietly with his thoughts, holding the woman who had changed his life. When it was time, she would go. There was danger in caring for her, fearing for the moment she would discover his deception. The beauty that had passed would be torn away, and he would be cold again. He inhaled slowly and cursed Nathaniel's plan to keep her safe.

He prayed that Nathaniel's team was nearing their goal, that the person making the threat would be stopped.

Morganna's soft thigh slid between his, her head resting on his shoulder comfortably. They belonged together, fitted together perfectly. Each time Jake's body met hers in passion, each time he had poured his essence into Morganna, his bond with her grew.

For Morganna the past night could mean an exploration, a temporary seduction of pleasure that would drift away like an autumn leaf swirling in the sunshine.

When she had held the child against her at the social, her expression of awe and tenderness had gently knocked his resistance aside. In that heartbeat, he envisioned her with his child and knew that she was his life. Jake wanted to treat her as his love, his wife . . . if only for the night.

Daylight skimmed across the room, catching in the black silky hair resting on his shoulder, and Jake's arms tightened possessively. He'd acted selfishly, wanting a small bit of her warmth to stow away, to salve the endless ache. He should tell her of Nathaniel, of the threats and his part in tucking her safely away.

Would she regret the night and their lovemaking?

He smiled into her hair, kissing her gently. Dianne was his first love, a sweet gentle person who had shared his life. Morganna, fiery, energetic and headstrong was Dianne's opposite. Morganna stirred beside him, inhaling softly, her breasts pressing against his side.

Jake closed his eyes as Morganna's slender hand crossed his chest. If Nathaniel didn't catch the maniac first . . . if Morganna was killed. . . . She inhaled sharply, then he realized he had been holding her too tightly. *Nothing could happen to her. He would keep her safe. Until she went, Morganna was his.*

As a modern woman, she might not like his acquisition of her. Or those terms. Jake stroked her body, sliding his palm down to cup and caress her femininity. He recognized the age-old, possessive gesture—a man claiming his mate.

Jake wasn't happy with his instinctive need for Morganna, nor the way she unraveled his passions. There was safety lurking in the shadows and scars waiting in the tomorrows. He'd fought to hide his desperation, his dark, shifting, fierce passions for her, leashing the power that he had never known for another woman.

She stirred at his side, lifting slightly, and for an instant Jake feared the regret that would follow. She blushed immediately, tugging the sheet up to her chin, but keeping her arm wrapped tightly around his side. He liked that, the soft anchor binding him to her. Propping her elbow on his chest, Morganna raised slightly. Those clear green eyes studied him carefully, and Jake clung to a precipice of fear. Would she deny him?

"I have honestly never slept so well," she whispered, bending to kiss him. Her fingers roamed his chest, and Jake's lids nearly closed with the sweet emotion piercing him. Morganna was a touching woman, one who absorbed textures though her fingertips and currently she was absorbing and enjoying him. "Thank you."

He chuckled at that, immediately relieved, and realized he had been holding his breath. "That's supposed to be my line."

"I like waking up to you," she said quietly, lying back in the circle of his arm to study him. Tracing his lips with her fingertips, Morganna's eyes darkened. "You're a very tender, delicious man, Jake Tallman. I didn't know—" Then she yawned and stretched at his side. "So this is what it's like," she murmured thoughtfully.

"Mmm." Jake didn't want to leave the moment, nor Morganna in his bed. He desperately wanted to tell her about Nathaniel, about his mission to the mountain.

Then Morganna moved quickly, agilely, pinning him with her soft body. "Was it all a dream, Jake? Will the daylight take it all away?" she asked urgently.

"Daylight makes the best loving time, Blossom," he returned, already slipping into her.

Her eyes widened, and her smile was delighted. "Oh, Jake. This is marvelous. It works better each time," she exclaimed.

The woman was quick, too agile and a fast learner, Jake decided two hours later. He frowned slightly, fighting the silly grin that kept returning. Her last cries echoed in his ear, and just the thought made him hard again. She was sleeping in his bed, looking more like a child than a woman who had spent the night and half the morning making love. At eleven in the morning Jake wanted to join her again, then resisted. With Tyree due in the afternoon, he wouldn't risk embarrassing Morganna.

He smiled again, filled with the warmth inside him and the sight of Morganna's bra hanging from the doorknob. Jake tucked it into his pocket as he read the note that was tacked to the door. Petey had mysterious errands and would return to feed the calves that night. Jake allowed her to sleep until noon, then returned to their bed.

Morganna threatened him darkly, refused to rouse and tugged a pillow over her head. Staking him to an ant hill sounded more convincing in Colorado's dry sweeping fields than her threats of keelhauling or feeding him by bits to sharks. He smiled at the threat of faxing him to Jupiter. She flopped on her stomach, still clutching the pillow. Jake ripped off the covers and swatted her backside gently. It was a perfect backside, he noted, soft and quivering beneath his caressing palm. His body reacted immediately, then Morganna lurched to her feet on the bed, holding the pillow to conceal her body and scowling at him. "If you ever swat me again, Jake, I shall have to retaliate. Don't ask me how, I don't know how. But I will."

Then she giggled and swatted him with the pillow. The novelty of a pillow fight with a woman stunned him at first. Then Morganna giggled again and leapt into his arms, pillow and all. Over it, she kissed him sweetly and whispered, "Don't look so shocked, Jake. I've just had my revenge."

Eight

Morganna huddled in the bath water, shielding her body from Jake's speculative glances in the steamy mirror. Sharing a bathroom with him while he shaved, his chest bare and his long jean-clad legs locked at the knee, was unnerving. When he turned from the mirror, she sank deeper in the sudsy water. "Tyree should arrive at any minute. Are you getting out of there?" he asked, patting his face dry with a towel.

When she blushed, holding the washcloth to her chest, Jake smiled tenderly and crouched by the tub. "Blossom, I've seen it all, remember?" Taking her palms, he pressed them to his lips, holding them against the hard bones of his face. Sunlight slid through the high window to touch his black hair, and the moment held a nuance of reverence as though Jake deeply valued her, cherished her. The emotion was startlingly new to Morganna, who found herself shivering, though she was very warm. Then, taking care, Jake brushed away a damp strand of hair from her cheek and ran his thumb across her sensitive lips. "You look well loved, Blossom—"

He lifted his head and listened. "Tyree just pulled up." He kissed her hard, then carefully closed the bathroom door behind him.

When Morganna entered the kitchen later, Jake plopped a huge sandwich in front of an angular boy almost as tall as himself. One look at Jake's dark expression, and Morganna realized that she had entered at a critical moment. Jake nodded curtly to her and pulled a chair out to seat her. The boy's eyes darted to Morganna, then up to Jake, and slowly he pushed back his chair and stood. He dipped his head, cleared his throat and muttered, "Ma'am."

"That's better." Jake placed a thick roast beef sandwich in front of her. "Morganna Larrimore, meet Tyree Lang. Tyree, this is the lady I've been telling you about."

The boy's wary expression, as though the world had dealt him a lifetime of pain, tugged at Morganna's heart. As darkly tanned as Jake, the boy's hair was long and greasy, tied at the nape of his neck by a beaded leather thong. The red flannel shirt he wore was clumsily mended with black running stitches. His legs were encased with dirty frayed jeans that topped boots with loose soles. He avoided Jake's hard stare as the older man jerked out a chair and sat.

Clearly the argument had just been heating up when she appeared, and Jake's rigid expression matched the boy's sullen one. "Eat that sandwich, Tyree," Jake bit out. "Drink your milk."

"I've been eating okay, Jake," the boy muttered, avoiding Jake's eyes. "All the right stuff."

"Sure you have. Beer and chips. You've been in a few fights, too, and spending your time hanging out at that rattrap hangout at the junction."

Tyree's eyes jerked up, his fury visible. "The other guys are there. We've got the place fixed up okay."

"Mike and Lopez. Probably Regan and Ole, right? Fine company."

Tyree half rose from his chair, his young face rigid with anger. Jake's eyes narrowed. "Put it down there," he ordered in a voice Morganna remembered easily.

She pushed her sandwich delicately around the plate, placing aside the layers of beef. "Stop that," Jake ordered sharply, his fingers sliding between hers. She sensed his sharp tone was more from frustration with the boy than with herself and remained quiet. However, in the future Jake would have to watch his tones with her.

Jake's hand stilled her fingers. "She does that when she's thinking," he informed the youth and caressed the back of her hand with his thumb. She noted that Jake was a caressing, cuddling, touching man as he continued, "The point is, Tyree, you're headed for trouble—"

"The Clover Leaf can afford the loss of a few calves, Jake," the boy returned hotly. "Mike said we could get a good price for them in Nimrod. There's a guy there that asks no questions—"

"That's enough," Jake said too quietly. "What about your education? Are you finishing your high school degree?"

"Nah. Dull stuff. Takes too much time, and there's nowhere to go after you put in all that time and work." He slid a glance at Morganna. "You don't have what it takes to stay here, lady. Life's tough and sailing down a nowhere street."

His words, shot with bitterness, caught Morganna broadside. Her life had been protected, her education and future secure despite the revolving stepmothers and their children. Her life with her father and Paul was always there. "There are ways to make your life better—"

"Sure." Tyree dropped the word like the proverbial cow pile, his young face suddenly old. "It all takes bucks. I came from nowhere and I'm going nowhere. So what if I pick up a few extra beeves along the way to make the going easier."

Jake inhaled sharply. "Tyree, I want you to live with me."

For an instant the boy's face softened, then his mouth turned down. "Man, I make my own way. Nobody carries me. You start with that paying for my education bit and I'm out of here. I know you'd have to sell off stock from that herd you're building or maybe mortgage again. No way. Tyree Lang doesn't bring nobody down.''

They ate in silence, and Jake filled a sack with food for Tyree, walking him out to the truck. When he returned, Morganna sensed his dark frustration. Then he saw her in the shadows, walked straight for her and kissed her hard as though he needed the contact. Morganna held him tightly, stroking his taut back until he lifted his head. ''It's like that here. I suppose it's like that in the cities. Kids on the prowl . . . I just happened to be one of the lucky ones.''

''It's a waste.''

''It's a matter of money. This area could use a good vo-tech school. People are working to survive and kids like Tyree are dropping through the slats every day. Adults can't leave their families to retrain for new job markets.''

Morganna leaned against him, listening to the comforting thud of his heart. ''You're helping.''

''When I can,'' Jake returned grimly. ''I'd like to see that vo-tech school become a reality. I've been working on it, and there has been a little interest, but it's going far too slowly. Every day, every month counts with a boy like Tyree.''

''In a way he's like my brother, Paul . . . uncertain of life. Tyree is fighting to find out who he is. My father is a very strong-minded individual, and Paul isn't able to stand up to him.'' Unused to sharing her troubled life with anyone, she glanced at Jake who nodded. An easy man to talk with, he listened carefully, and when he acted, he acted with his heart, stripped of whatever false stigmas civilization placed on manhood. His large hand held hers, a gesture that she could grow to love.

An hour and forty minutes later, Jake's open hand slapped the truck's dusty, cluttered dashboard. He scowled at her from the passenger side of the vehicle. ''How can shifting gears be so difficult?''

Morganna uncurled her aching fingers from the huge steering wheel. She pressed her lips together and inhaled slowly. "Perhaps it's the teacher, Jake," she muttered very sweetly. "You're not very patient."

He stared at her blankly. "I've taught several people to drive. Women...kids.... *I have patience, lots of it,*" he said in a soft roar. "You're making this more difficult than it is."

"Cars weren't meant to have clutches or 'H' patterned gear shifts," she argued logically and wondered if she imagined the tender, gentle man who could devastate her with that reluctant, boyish grin.

Jake leveled a scowl at her, and she drummed her fingers on the wheel. She would not allow him to upset her further. "It's hard to concentrate on all these doodads with you constantly yelling at me," she returned, defending her honor as a quick learner.

"Yelling?" he repeated in another soft roar. He rammed his fingers through his hair and shook his head disbelievingly. *"Who wouldn't yell when the transmission is getting ripped out of his truck?"*

Jake shifted suddenly, and his knee bumped the glove box, which popped open and her pantyhose pooled onto his jeans. Jake stared at them as though they were snakes, his fist crushing them. The evidence of her lovemaking with a man who had just been yelling at her was too much. She resented Jake's marred patience and the way she wanted him to cuddle her. She resented the tears burning at her lids...she resented Fanny Olingberg's frothy blond curls and experience in cuddling— "Give me those," she ordered, jerking them away and stuffing them into the jacket she had borrowed from Jake.

She liked wearing his clothes. They made her feel a part of him. She loved the sensitive man he could be.

She hated him as a driving instructor.

"Okay," Jake said slowly, running his thumb along the toe of the pantyhose leg that escaped her pocket, rambling across the seat to him. "You're all worked up—"

She turned to him slowly. "I am never worked up when I'm with anyone else. You're implying that I'm not in control . . . I am."

"Uh-huh," Jake said warily and glanced at her fingers drumming the steering wheel. "Look. Maybe teaching you to drive a truck without power steering is too much. Maybe the standard transmission was too difficult—"

"*What?*" She retrieved the pantyhose leg, stuffing it into her pocket. "Have I ever told you, Jake Tallman, that in some ways you remind me of my father? I am currently at war with him."

"Simmer down, Blossom. Not everyone is equipped to drive a truck like this—"

"Simmer? Simmer?" she asked in rapid fire order. "Are you implying that I am losing my temper, Jake? *Why would I do that when you've taught so many successful drivers before me?*"

For the first time Jake was uncertain how to approach the smoldering female glaring at him, waiting for him to continue. The wrong word could end the relationship they had just begun. Morganna was a bright businesswoman; she would realize every person had certain areas of weakness. Jake moved his mouth and found himself saying, "Maybe we should skip the driving lessons. . . ."

Her eyebrows arced high, and her fingertips drummed the steering wheel. She very carefully tossed him a verbal hot potato. "You are saying in so many words, that I am incapable of learning. I *can* drive an automatic shift, you know," she added with a soft threat.

While Jake mentally bounced that burning potato and considered the alternatives, the volatile female gripping the truck's steering wheel watched him intently. Now that Morganna was committed to him, he had certain rights. One of them was anticipating her warm, agile body next to his for the remainder of her stay. That incentive alone made him clamp his lips closed until he found a way to tell her about Nathaniel's request.

He was a very greedy man where Morganna was concerned.

"I see," Morganna said meaningfully after a tense minute had passed. With that she stomped on the clutch, searched for first gear, found second and smiled nastily at him. "There. It's easy, see? Any idiot can drive a standard gearshift."

Jake sat quietly in his corner of the cab, his fingers gripping his thighs while the truck lurched to the house. Morganna turned off the key, glared at him while the truck sputtered and died, then stalked into the house. She slammed the door after her.

Jake unsuccessfully tried to uncurl his fingers from his thighs, which had started aching. He forced his unsteady hands to open and shifted the abused truck into its proper gear. He studied that firmly closed door and decided he should check the calves in the barn.

That night Jake followed Nathaniel's directions that Petey had taken over the phone during the infamous driving lesson. While Morganna was taking her bath, Jake rode Black Jack to the end of the lane. He found Nathaniel's black stretch limousine sitting at the end of the lane and tied Black Jack to a fence post.

Lounging in the lighted interior, Nathaniel sipped a beer while he worked on the papers from his briefcase, which was open on the seat beside him. He took a beer from the refrigerated unit and nodded for Jake to sit opposite him. The window between the driver and the spacious interior that was loaded with luxuries slid closed and the chauffeur continued to read his newspaper.

Jake twisted off the lid and drank deeply. "This is a cow pile," he stated flatly.

"My people are closing in on a man named Winslow Ames. Rita picked a choice team of sleuths. Her updates are detailed. He skipped just an hour before them in New York, leaving a trail up to Toronto. They're up there now, picking up leads." In the lighted interior, Nathaniel scanned Jake's face carefully. "Thank you for getting her off that moun-

tain. I made the mistake of telling her that wasn't any place
for a woman. I should have known she'd jump straight for
it with that idiot female bonding thing she's into—''

The chauffeur knocked on the window and pointed into
the night. "Someone's walking up the road. Looks like a
boy with a big dog, maybe a wolf, following him."

The door jerked open, and Morganna slid into the cab.
Dirty sounded a long, mournful howl nearby. She sat on the
seat, a distance away from her father and facing Jake.
"How charming. A rendezvous of the plotters, hatching a
scheme under the moon.... Warlocks in a limo—that's absolutely fascinating." Her gaze swung to Jake, and she fas-
tidiously removed her jeaned legs from between his long
ones. "Tell me, Jake...how do you know my father?"

Nathaniel growled and stuffed the papers inside the
briefcase, snapping it shut. He watched grimly while Morganna retrieved it and flipped through his paperwork,
marking out lines and making notations along the way.
When she jotted a few notes on his tablet and returned the
case, Nathaniel said, "It's a long story."

"I've got the time. Heavens, it's oh...maybe eight hours
before I have to feed the chickens. They're baseline entry in
the ranching business. I haven't worked up to the real livestock level yet." Morganna glanced at Jake's beer and
reached to the cabinet to pour a glass of very expensive
champagne. Jake watched the deliberate, elegant movements of her hands and decided that he would sit out the
argument between the Larrimores. Nathaniel was on his
own. After a sip, she smiled tightly. "Don't tell me, Pops.
You've added a limo delivery for beer-thirsty cowboys in the
middle of nowhere to the corporation's fast-food services."

"Dammit, Morganna. If you hadn't decided on that
scatterbrained, bonding expedition, none of this would have
happened. The sensible women returned with the helicopter—but, oh, no, not my daughter. The situation was critical, and since I knew Jake, I asked for his help."

Jake carefully noted that Larrimore omitted the details
concerning the threats to Morganna's life.

"I see," she said thoughtfully, and in the dimly lit interior her face was too pale, a fleeting shadow of pain darkening her eyes as she looked at Jake. A sudden wrench of pain slammed into him as her bottom lip trembled for a heartbeat, then her mouth firmed. "Lovely. So the king sent his knight to save me."

Nathaniel glanced uneasily at Jake and slouched in his leather seat. "Oh, hell. She's starting that checkmate manure. Has to do with her theory that business and chess are alike."

She sipped the champagne, studying the bubbles. "Your confidence in me is amazing, father. So the two of you big strong men decided that I couldn't fend for myself—"

"That's enough," Jake said quietly, noting the slight tremble of her hand as she replaced the empty glass.

"Enough? Not by far," Morganna returned in a dangerously soft tone. "You see there are things that I can do well, Jake...quite well. When I decide just how I will handle this situation, you'll find out."

"I don't like the sound of that," Nathaniel stated darkly.

"Too bad, Pops. The cards have been played. Jake has kindly obliged you by keeping me occupied." Tears shimmered in her eyes before she blinked them away.

Jake inhaled, placed his beer aside and kept his eyes on Morganna's pale face. "Your father is worried for your life, Morganna. A man named Winslow Ames is stalking you. If Nathaniel's people don't find Ames before he locates you, you're safer here than in a city. A stranger will be spotted the minute he drives into town."

"Winslow Ames? Oh, him. You've got to be kidding. I dealt with him six months ago. When did this happen?" Morganna's wide eyes jerked to Nathaniel.

His grim stare met Jake's, who asked, "Why does he want to kill her?"

"Am I to be included in the male Society for the Protection of Poor, Defenseless Morganna Larrimore?" she asked tightly. "I'll tell his motive. Eleven months ago, Winslow wanted to date me, apparently with the grand plan of marriage. I refused to have anything to do with him, and he was incensed. He was a board member—my father's 'yes' man, until he developed his own ideas. Winslow made deals on my behalf, without my knowledge, that were severely dangerous to the environment. A whole species of cute little fish would vanish if his project were activated. I blocked his schemes and fired him and his plotters on the spot. He lost a bundle of money on the project. Winslow flew into a rage and threatened my life within the hour. I informed him that I wouldn't tolerate, nor be frightened by his vengeance. I also told him that if he didn't make his split with Larrimore's look like a resignation—for the sake of our business image, and because I didn't want problems from you, Father—I would personally see that word about his underhanded tactics was spread from here to hell.''

"Good God, Morganna. You mean he threatened you and you didn't say a word?'' Nathaniel yelled. He waved a hand when the chauffeur slid open the window and peered into the spacious interior. "Close it...I thought Winslow quit because of a better position, Morganna.''

"It's not the first time I've handled threats. You need protection from the hardships of business periodically. In some instances you are far too fragile and volatile, Father. At the time I didn't want you hurt or shaken by your choice of an absolute nincompoop,'' she returned stiffly, searching Jake's face.

In the shadows a tear slid from her lashes before Morganna swiped it away. Her bottom lip trembled in her pale face, her eyes large and wounded. "You kept me here—entertained me—on my father's instructions.''

Jake leaned forward to take her cold, trembling hands, and Morganna jerked them away, her eyes fierce now, slashing at him. "Misled and entertained me to keep me away from Larrimores—''

"To keep you safe." Jake ached for her, wanted to hold her and kiss away the stark pain of her expression.

"You could have told me...two men keeping secrets from me and deciding my fate,'' she whispered unevenly. "It boggles the mind. Either one of you didn't consider me capable of making decisions that concern my life. Protecting poor little Morganna."

"Hell, Morganna. That fiasco of women bonding on a primitive mountain was sheer—" Nathaniel began and stopped when Morganna's green eyes pinned him.

She looked at Jake, her expression grim. "I am furious. Please consider my resignation. I'm taking the limo home."

"Not by a long shot." He would protect Morganna as long as he could.

Morganna flushed. "Jake, you—"

"You've agreed to help out at the ranch. You're staying put."

Nathaniel scanned Morganna's hot face, her furious stare and Jake's set expression. Her father's handsome, craggy face lit up when he noted for the first time that Morganna was wearing a man's large shirt beneath her jacket and the rolled-up cuffs of jeans much to large for her. "Something important brewing that I should know about?"

"Nothing," Morganna answered flatly, glaring at Jake. Her hair swirled around her face as she turned to her father. "You've challenged my honor, Pops. In my place you would be considering methods of retaliation."

Nathaniel slashed out his hand in a chopping motion. "It's not the same thing—"

"But it is. I'm taking that bus in the morning, Jake."

Jake fought his racing fear and struck out with a challenge. "Tyree said you wouldn't make it. You owe me those two weeks, Blossom."

"Blossom?" Nathaniel repeated with a happy lilt to his raspy voice. Then softer, tasting the name on his tongue and liking it. "Blossom."

"Don't get any ideas, Father. It's some archaic reference to Jake's perception of what a woman should be—soft, sweet and pliable." Morganna's fiery green eyes were huge in her pale face. "Surely you don't expect me to continue."

When he nodded, her slender fingers curled into a fist and Nathaniel watched with interest, his eyes gleaming as Morganna slid agilely out the door.

Jake caught her easily a few strides down the dirt lane. He glimpsed Nathaniel's grin in the half-opened window a moment before it closed, the limousine gleaming as it slid over the moonlit highway.

Morganna's fist caught him in the eye as he turned her. Sweeping her against him, Jake grunted softly as she squirmed. "Blossom..."

Her tears were warm on his lips, her skin smooth and chilled by the night. "I want you with me," he said roughly, meaning it, holding her closer. When she stilled slightly, her body taut and trembling, he stroked her hair. He refused to release her, rocking her in his arms, while terror ricocheted through his chest.

She sniffed against his shoulder, refusing to bend. "You could have told me that my father sent you.... How do you know him?"

Jake's thoughts skimmed back to another woman and found the pain had dimmed. "Your father was the first one to find my wife's car. He risked his life to rescue Dianne and my unborn son. He did what he could to make her comfortable in those last moments of her life."

"I see." She softened, her hands drumming on his waist. "Your injured ankle seems to have healed."

Jake nuzzled the silky curve of her cheek. "I wanted you with me," he repeated, meaning it. "Are you staying or not?"

The heat of her face enchanted him, then a shudder ripped through her curved body, and Jake gathered her closer. "Oh, Jake, why did you make love to me?"

His heart pounded, his body chilled. The wrong answer could cost him dearly. "I made love to you because I wanted you more than I wanted my next breath...."

Her body softened slightly. The busy fingers slid along his belt and Jake sucked in his breath. "I trusted you, Jake. Right now I'm uncertain about anything, except that I am too angry to make a clear decision about anything. I don't like the idea of my father and you in cahoots over my welfare. The thought is mind-boggling. I'll consider the matter and get back to you."

Walking away from him in the moonlight, Morganna seemed very small, very vulnerable. Jake's stomach contracted sharply, his fists aching at his sides.

Tyree grinned, his face losing the tough lines as Morganna sat behind the steering wheel of his old truck. "Lady, you need me," he said smugly. "This is going to be an easy way to earn money... it may take a *long* time."

Morganna pushed in the clutch, inhaled ten times to steady her frazzled nerves, then cautiously slid the floor stick into first gear. She had remained awake and tossing till dawn. If only she hadn't called Else and asked her to have Tyree meet her when Jake rode off into the mountains with Dirty, seeking a lost cow and calf.

For the past week she'd circled Jake's deception, weighing it. She ached to cross an invisible line, to ease his wary expression—though it was usually grim when she cooked, and he seemed in a constant cycle of pick up and straighten. She wanted a relationship with Jake, but there the concept became blurred, confused. He'd rescued and deceived her. Then her father had definitely breached her life and her honor demanded revenge. She would never forget the warlock convention in the moonlit limo.

Gently, so gently, she concentrated on Tyree's instructions and began releasing the clutch. They were sneaky little things, he'd explained, and had certain pressure points that varied from vehicle to vehicle. They couldn't be trusted, he assured her. At magical points—the clutch on release and the gas petal pressed slowly down—the two collided, engaged and the wheels would move, the engine would rev. She shot a look at Tyree, who was still grinning. "I'd really like to try this with the motor running."

He flicked a straw from his sleeve, and she noted that he was clean and his clothes, though worn had been washed. "Sorry. No way. You're not up to it."

"Will I be soon?" she asked hopefully, then frowned at Tyree's smirk.

"Like I said. This is going to be easy money. Run through that again. Shift into first, then second, third and fourth."

"Tyree, I really would love to turn on the key. I'm certain I could do much better with a live motor. Please?"

"Hey. I've got a bundle in this rig. It's tuned like a maestro's violin string or Wendy Beauchamps on a Friday night. No way are you getting a real live motor yet. By the way, did you ever find out where Jake got that black eye about a week ago?"

She curled her fingers into a fist, remembering the impact of it on Jake's eye. "Bumped into a post," he'd snapped at Petey the next morning. The leathery cowboy's smirk grew each time Jake glared at him. Jake's bruised eye reminded Morganna of her lack of control and the reason for her anger.

When she didn't answer Tyree's question, he shrugged and continued, "Lady, you've got to love the gears, feel them out real slow, study 'em, find where they live and then ease 'em where you want 'em."

Tyree shifted, settled into the seat and dreamily stroked the dashboard. "See, Morg. This is how it is. There's fine tuning involved. You have to meet this prime piece of machine on an equal basis. You tell it what you want, show it what you can do, and the gears mesh . . . action. It takes a firm hand, guts and love to run a work of art like this."

Morganna stared at Tyree and blinked. The way the boy spoke about his car was the way she wanted to experience Jake. "Tell me that part again, Tyree."

In Dan's ranch office that afternoon, Morganna's fingers flew over the computer's keyboard. Hannah sipped tea while she watched from the safety of an overstuffed chair. Morganna inhaled, straightened, checked her paper list against the computer screen, then exited and turned the unit off. "I've tapped into the office's computer mainframe, checked up on progress reports and posted a memo to my father. We have an appointment next week for a very serious discussion about exactly who is in charge of my life."

Morganna moved agilely, pacing the floor of the sunlit, wood-paneled room.

"Raspberry leaf tea?" Hannah asked, pouring from an old-fashioned pottery tea pot into a mug. In her living room, Jasmine's Every Other Wednesday Afternoon Ladies Quilting Circle hummed away, stitching a beautifully patterned quilt over a quilting frame. The newest subject of the circle was Jake's obvious attraction to a "city woman." The probing, friendly inquiries were featherlight and very obvious to Morganna, who couldn't stop blushing. "They mean well," Hannah said, noting Morganna's frown at the door. "I hope you don't mind. It's just that we all love Jake, and he's been so alone. We're all so pleased that you've entered his life."

Hannah picked up a tiny pair of leather booties with fringes and swung them gently. "Jake made these. He's artistic and very sensitive about his talents. He has a beautiful sense of color and texture. He told Dan that your skin was like white rose petals warmed by sunlight."

Hannah frowned and smoothed the booties with her fingertips. "One of the foster parents, zealous about meeting realities, considered Jake's artistic talents to be the work of the devil. Jake barely survived that brute's heavy-handed tactics. By the time Mrs. Blaylock located Jake in that boys' home, the other children had tormented him mercilessly. Some of his talent came back. But you can see it surface every now and then. It's in his beaded leather work, in the way he stares at sunsets or children, or in the way he touches . . . light, caressing strokes as if finding what lies beneath. He's a natural storyteller. He'd be a marvelous father."

Morganna jerked her eyes away from the booties, fighting the flutter of pain for Jake the child. Then she thought about Jake's reaction to her baby maker lists. He'd never qualified for the husband list. "He collaborated with my father and interrupted my bonding with nature and meditation. Jake and my father have decided that I can't manage." Morganna perched on the desk and studied her boots, her fingers drumming the pottery mug. Though Jake felt obligated to Nathaniel, there was still the matter of lovemaking and tender, sweet kisses. Deceiving and bedding her required an exquisite revenge. "There are gears to be shifted."

"What?" Hannah asked quizzically and grinned when Morganna blushed. "The Blaylock men are notorious for assuming that they know what is best for their lady loves, Morganna. There is no doubt that Jake is—" She tactfully avoided the word *love*. "—enchanted by you. Why do you think he took you to the old adobe? Because he sensed that you were meant for him."

"'Lady love'," Morganna repeated darkly, regretting every last gasp of pleasure Jake had heard from her. "I haven't put together the entire picture yet. But I will and prove to Jake that I am his equal on any level."

She looked at Hannah. "I've ordered information on the subject of sensuality. Jake has the advantage there, and I don't like it. I want to see him coming and know what to expect. Until now he's had the upper hand."

Hannah's lips curled slowly in an amused smile. "Research never hurts."

Morganna slid her gaze to Jake and Dan, who were riding side by side, studying Dan's herd. She pushed away the ache that had clung to her throughout the night.

"Your father and Jake were worried about your safety," Hannah offered gently.

Were Jake's sweet kisses and hungry, tender lovemaking a product of her father's scheme? Morganna wondered, her heart tearing a little.

She had to prove to him and herself that she could meet him on any level before she walked away.

Morganna studied Jake through the window, tapped her pottery mug and balanced her thoughts. Suddenly she realized she was speaking aloud, "I don't fit in."

"You can stitch a quilt square as well as anyone. You even impressed Sarah Langtree, and she is a demon if a stitch is turned wrong."

Morganna studied the basket of quilting pieces given to her by Hannah and Else. She touched a scrap of white material and wished she had known the quiet, shy, uncertain boy who had worn it. Elizabeth Blaylock had fashioned Jake's first shirt as a member of the Blaylock family to make him feel like one of her sons. According to Else, Jake was never comfortable with that family love, always circling on the perimeter and escaping when it reached too close.

As a man Jake didn't fit the picture of that endearing, lonely boy. He had tampered with her emotions and her pride and he needed a fervent tap on those hard knuckles.

She shivered when she remembered his intimate, possessive cupping of her femininity. Morganna resented the deep, restful sleep after their lovemaking. She resented the taut nerves and sleepless nights since. She resented the need to physically attack him, to waylay him in the barn and— There the image changed a bit and shifted back into the explosive passion she wished to use on Jake. Dark, fierce looks wouldn't frighten her away. She would realign those confused images, blend them into a comprehensive picture and initiate steps for revenge.

Hannah touched Morganna's eyes and smiled. "Don't tell me you're walking away from Jake without settling the matter between you."

"I wouldn't think of it. I just haven't figured out the p's and q's yet. I am going to disintegrate him." She ignored Hannah's rippling laughter.

Nine

"*A vocational school? You're doing what?*" her father yelled from his Kansas City office.

Morganna doodled on her pad, frowned at the heart and scored a deep, black *X* across it. She was finally alone, her thoughts taking shape. After lunch Petey, Tyree and Jake had left to tend the cattle. Morganna had checked her office for messages and waited for Rita's special delivery messenger.

She had puttered, dusted Jake's beautiful small carvings of animals and prowled through the scraps of cloth from the Blaylock family. She traced the quilting square she had fashioned from Fay Dupres's triangular pattern. Here was Jake's white Sunday shirt, Logan's wedding shirt. The red calico cotton was Missy Blaylock's dress for Jasmine's Old Tyme Days Rodeo and Fandango. A scrap of pink cotton, dotted with tiny rosebuds had belonged to Fancy, Logan's daughter, and a variety of scraps remained from Else's dresses. A brilliant yellow had been used in a daffodil costume for the Jasmine Grade School Play.

While she had cut and fashioned the bits of cloth to form a loose square pattern, Morganna had listed her priorities on a pad at her side. She'd used the method for difficult problems, and when she had sorted the collection of notes, the answer fell smoothly into place.

"You can afford it, Pops," she murmured sweetly, lifting a scrap of heart-spattered cloth to the sunlight pouring into the kitchen. She doodled a row of hearts on her pad. "Think of all those unused thousands as a tax break. By the way, I'll need a camper trailer and a first-class computer with a modem. I'll begin the first week of June. The project should be ready for the new school year by August. Count on contributing computers and modems for the outreach students, who can't make class because of snow. Of course, when the students link their computers to the one at the school by telephone, Larrimore Corporation will foot the bill. I think some students might be able to get their high school degree that way, too."

"You're out for revenge, Morganna. You're taking the bread right out of my mouth. Taking the shirt right off my back . . . tossing away every profit we've just earned in acquiring that new computer factory. You've finally proved me right. A woman's emotional brain has no place in decision-making levels. You'll destroy everything we've built. The Larrimores will starve."

"Very dramatic, Father. It may work in the boardroom or with a wife or two, but you're dealing with me now. Call Stan in our real estate section and have him purchase a land parcel. It's located on the intersection five miles south of Jasmine. It's called 'the junction,' and the vacant feed store and gas station can be easily renovated." She'd noted the building's possibilities when Jake had driven her to Dan Blaylock's ranch, the Flying H.

"Dammit, Morganna. We're in the business of real estate, malls, electronics and making a dab of profit from grabbing up dying markets and incorporating them into our structure. Benefiting communities through education is not one of our goals. We are not in the business of starting up vocational schools.''

''We are now,'' she returned before replacing the receiver. What she lacked in certain domestic and ranching skills, she compensated for by doing what she did best— building a business, establishing connections, reaching out and creating a successful venture. All she needed was a telephone and a computer.

By doing what she knew best and waving it under Jake's and her father's collective noses, she could gain that equal footing. Only then could she have complete, glorious revenge and be able to walk away with her pride.

There were larger issues at hand than Winslow Ames's threats. There was the matter of trust. While she expected her father's tactics, Jake's keeping secrets from her while sharing her bed in mind-blowing beauty was not permissible. She dashed away a tear with the back of her hand and sniffed. Heavy-handed tyrants, the two of them.

While Jake had touched her with reverence and tenderness, he was responsible for unleashing certain primitive emotions. She could never forgive him for that. Nor would she play second best to a wife he had loved deeply. Nor would she tolerate being stuffed into a compact, neat little memory, as Jake tucked away his leather projects or his carvings. And darn him, he'd given her a taste of the cuddles.

The messenger arrived promptly at one o'clock, and Morganna ripped open the cardboard box filled with books, magazines and a clip file from a secretary, Mary Ann. Though Mary Ann refused to work with Morganna, her style was appealing. Plain in appearance, sexuality had steamed from Mary Ann when she'd been hunting the man who eventually became her husband. She attributed her new appeal to a clip file consisting of articles from magazines and tips from other women. Only Rita had knowledge of the secret weapon and had persuaded Mary Ann to share it this one time.

Morganna munched on the bacon she had cooked at breakfast. It matched her well-done toast perfectly, and Jake and Petey both marveled at her new expertise, though they didn't eat very much.

Mary Ann's clip file fascinated Morganna, and she was startled to find Tyree leering at the material she had scattered over the table. "Way to go, Morg. Neat stuff." He leered while leafing through A Modern Woman's Guide to Fostering Intimate Relations and The Contemporary Woman Hunts a Mate. He frowned, studying a passage then asked, "Hey, Morg. So I can count on my...ah...my date carrying protection with her, right? I mean if we...uh...you know?" His finger ran along a line. "Hey, what's this part about 'the assertive woman hunts her mate'?"

"Give me that." Tyree frowned when Morganna jerked the book away, her face burning. She stuffed the material into the box, lugged it to her bedroom and crammed it under her bed.

With his head lowered in the opened refrigerator, Tyree said, "Jake wants you to pack sandwiches and something to drink and bring it out to Petey and him. They're working the cattle in the north pasture."

"That fits my plans perfectly. I'll drive," Morganna snapped, tossing bread, the ever-present lunch meat and lettuce into an ice cooler. She leveled a meaningful stare at Tyree. "If you say anything about my reading material, you're dead."

Tyree smirked. "It'll cost. I'll get back to you. But you're not driving my rig. Not with a running motor."

To her surprise Dirty hopped up into Tyree's pickup and sat between the two humans like a pleasant chum sharing the short, bouncy ride across a wide field. He tolerated Morganna's petting hand, but laid his muzzle on Tyree's shoulder.

"Oh, my goodness," Morganna whispered when they approached Jake and Petey. Dressed in full chaps, Jake reined Black Jack to a hard stop, the rope circling the calf's neck snapped taut, and the calf flopped to the earth, bawling. Jake threw his legs to the ground at a run, whipped a small rope from his waist and wrapped it around the calf's four feet in a matter of three seconds or less.

The calf bawled, its mother milled and mooed nearby and Petey did something ghastly to its ear while Jake held its head. "Marking them," Tyree explained quietly.

When the men moved to the rear of the calf, Morganna gasped, forgetting her grand plans for revenge instantly. "What are they doing now?"

"Uh...uh, jeez, you don't want to know."

"But I do. First they maul the poor thing, try to break its neck, then they hurt its ears and now what?"

The boy cleared his throat. "Uh...call it a sex change."

But Morganna was running toward Jake. He glanced at her, muttered something to Petey and turned, stripping off his gloves as she threw herself into his arms. "Oh, Jake, please don't hurt that calf anymore.... Please?"

She clung to him, shuddering, her arms wrapped tightly around his neck. "Oh, Jake, please don't," she whispered into his throat. "How can you be so brutal to such an innocent animal?"

"Blossom..." Then taking a deep breath, Jake picked her up and carried her back to Tyree's pickup. "It's what happens on a ranch, Blossom," he said, frowning as he wiped away her tears with his thumbs and bent to kiss her damp lashes.

"Oh, man..." Tyree muttered in disgust while Dirty howled.

Petey yelled for help, and Jake shot a glance over his shoulder. "Take her home, Tyree."

Morganna unclenched her fingers from Jake's denim jacket and ran her forearm across her damp face, drying it. Looking very tall and rugged, a western cowboy in his element, Jake slapped his dusty hat against his thigh and ran his hand through his hair. "This was a mistake. She doesn't belong out here now. Take her home," he repeated grimly. "Stay with her."

On the way to the ranch house, she sniffed and muttered about male bestiality to Dirty who listened and to Tyree, who didn't. Tyree worked in the barn, while Morganna searched the fields for signs of Jake and Petey. To keep busy she cut quilt pieces, then found Petey's famed tortilla recipe. Tyree stayed close, popping in and out of the house. He shot wary glances at her puttering in the kitchen.

When Jake and Petey returned after dark, she had made seventy-two tortillas and three neatly stitched quilting squares. Petey probed the tall stack of burned, thick round pancakes and asked, "What's these critters?"

Still miffed at Jake for brutalizing calves, Morganna resented how delicious he looked in chaps and a wary, defensive scowl. He handed her a bouquet of wildflowers and when her eyes filled with tears, he kissed her. That quick, hard kiss immobilized her while he entered the bathroom to take a shower. When she could find her breath, she whispered unevenly, "Oh, Petey. How sweet of him... I've never had a wildflower bouquet. They are gorgeous."

"There's bugs on 'em," he stated flatly, then sneezed. "Hurt my back bending over to pick 'em. Fool waste of time, but Jake wanted to. Better put 'em in a jar of water before they wilt."

"I love them, bugs and all," she whispered, cradling them to her.

Petey shuffled his worn boots. "They're like you. Sweet. Fresh. Good."

Morganna nuzzled a stalk of bluebells. "Why, Petey, that's almost romantic."

Petey's leathered face turned rosy. "No, it ain't at all," he snapped. "Romance is for young bloods and idiots. A feller gets past that stage and goes on to more mental endeavors. That's why Jake sent for you, you know. 'Cause he missed you. Then he got riled at himself 'cause he did. Then he got madder at himself 'cause you got so worked up. He figures you're a delicate little bud of a woman who needs protecting from life's rough spots."

Shaking his head and muttering, Petey quickly cooked meat and bean sauce and chopped lettuce, tomatoes and onions for her tortillas. Tyree probed at the tortillas, tried to break one in his hands and failed. He slapped it hard on the side of the counter and the tortilla cracked loudly. "Man, I don't know. Breaking teeth is serious business."

"They'll soften up with the sauce. I made it runny," Petey muttered, glancing sympathetically at Morganna. "Reckon if she spent the time to cook 'em, we'll eat them."

"Yeah...uh...they probably taste better than they look...uh...I just remembered, the guys asked me to come over to the junction tonight. See you, Morg."

"I'll save one for you," Morganna offered cheerfully. When Tyree's pickup sailed off into the night, Dirty began to howl mournfully.

Jake and Petey ate in grim silence, saturating their tortillas in liberal amounts of sauce. Morganna picked at hers and decided that a meat, lettuce and tomato salad was all she needed. She'd discovered that eating a heavy meal before delivering a concept to the board always made her queasy. She tossed out, "I'll be staying the summer," just as a bug dropped from a delicate spray of blue bells into Petey's juicy salsa, meat and bean sauce.

The muscles in Jake's newly shaven jaw paused, then began to move slowly as he continued chewing. She watched with interest as he swallowed heavily and drank several sips of water. Petey tried to swallow, muttered something around the clump of tortilla and stepped outside for a minute. "Forgot to turn off the light in the barn. It draws bugs. They bite," he explained when he returned. He scanned the stacked tortillas, jerked an empty bread sack from a drawer and began stuffing them into it. "For the freezer. Never know when we might need these little jewels."

Petey cleared the table, placed small glasses of red wine in front of Jake and Morganna. He surveyed the bouquet, adjusted a delicate fuchsia-colored bloom to the light, and reached into the kitchen cabinets to extract two fat candles, which he lit. Then experimenting with the light, he slid them into different positions. Straightening, he tilted his head one way then another, moved to stand at the end of the table and surveyed his handiwork like an artist creating a picture. Then Petey eased Morganna's chair a bit closer to Jake's. "There. That's good," he said in a pleased tone, grinned and excused himself for the night. A second later he jerked open the door, grinned briefly at them, then clicked off the overhead light, leaving them drenched in candlelight.

"How's that again?" Jake asked softly. "You're staying the summer?"

She nodded. She wanted him to see her coming, to watch every step of her progress. "I've started a project nearby. I'll be living on-site."

"Project?" Jake's big hand wrapped around her drumming fingers. She tried to jerk away and failed. "You're not staying by yourself," Jake stated flatly without waiting for an answer.

That royally male tone brought Morganna's eyebrows upward. "I beg your pardon?"

They circled each other for the next week. Jake's angular features tightened with tension, and Morganna fought tears at every turn. He flicked stealthy glances at her, and though she sensed he wanted to say something important to her, Jake snapped at Petey. Morganna resented her sleepless nights and the dark circles under her eyes. Looming in her resentment pot was the knowledge that she had never slept so deeply—when she could sleep—as the night spent in Jake's arms.

The last week of May, Morganna jammed her gear into her duffel bag and sat on the front porch until a truck bearing the Larrimore logo collected her. While the driver waited, she kissed Petey's leathery cheek, then her eyes slashed up to Jake. "See you," she said airily.

Petey muttered and shielded the tear oozing from his lids by picking up Curds. Jake stood back, looking very arrogant in his western hat, shirt and chaps. "Yes, you will," he answered quietly. "We're not done."

She smiled tightly. "True. We're not. Count on it."

At seven the next morning, Jake jerked open the trailer door and stepped inside. Seated at the tiny table, Morganna looked up from the computer and her notes on the project. Tyree's pickup had followed her at a distance when she'd left Jake's ranch, and the boy had stayed near the junction building. Obviously he had reported to Jake, who had chosen to appear before she could wash away the effects of the old building's cobwebs and dust. "Welcome to my world. I've been expecting you.... Next time, please knock first," she said, her hand inviting him to look as he pleased.

"That lock isn't worth—" Jake snapped his mouth closed and tossed his hat to her couch. Wary and uncomfortable, Jake bristled with challenges and looked like heaven. Beneath the light denim jacket, he wore a pink and cream plaid western style-shirt, neatly tucked into those long, narrow jeans he filled so well. "You're up early."

Morganna tucked her outline for the seduction of Jake beneath her idea sketches for the building. She had spent the sleepless night cramming with Mary Ann's clip file. She would have preferred snuggling to Jake's hard warm body, which now filled the cramped interior of the camper. "I'm an early riser when working on an exciting project. By the way, Dirty howled all night. Tyree's stake-out really wasn't necessary. Winslow Ames—the rat who created this mess originally—is slinking in some hole in Miami. Rita is keeping me posted on the developments."

Jake's scowl challenged her, and she shifted restlessly, watching a fuchsia-colored bloom fall from her wilted wildflower bouquet. It fluttered from a high shelf to rest on Jake's gleaming black hair. "My father will be calling. Rita says he's getting worked up to swoop. Try to keep the level of warlocks meeting in a black limo at midnight to a minimum, will you?"

While Jake chewed on that, she tapped her pencil on the pad and resented how beautiful he was, standing tall and wary, cleanly shaved and scented of soap and after-shave. The angular beauty of his face startled her, as did the way his broad shoulders loomed in the small enclosure. The pearl snaps of his shirt begged to be ripped open, to reveal the triangular patch of hair beneath. According to one clipped article, savagery lurked in the female breast when stimulated by an attractive male. Morganna decided her savagery was at the red-hot level. She noted he wore his polished dress boots and that he carried a small gift, wrapped with a pink bow, which he tossed to the couch. "Okay. I'll bite. Tyree says you're ruining the junction building next door. He's grief-stricken, muttering about 'bygone days.' What is the project?"

Jake jerked open the doors to the cramped bedroom and dinky bathroom. A frothy negligee spilled to his boots and Jake jerked back, dislodging a peach-colored bra, which shared the same nail as a calendar. The bra fluttered lazily to the negligee. He stared at the lacy jumble grimly, swooped and retrieved them in a death grip and slammed them to her unmade bed. He shot her a grim, accusing glare and closed the doors with his boot. Though Morganna had used campers on other development sites, she wasn't prepared for Jake's rugged masculinity filling the small space. She slid Mary Ann's clip file for one project beneath a thick notebook and shrugged. "I've decided that you are right. That Jasmine does need a vocational school, and I'm developing one."

"I see," Jake said, his gaze sliding down her sweatshirt, camouflage pants and boots, then brushing, lingering on her breasts on the way back up to her face. He drew a cobweb from her hair. "So you're making your stand."

"Something like that." She desperately wanted to know what was in the intriguing little package.

As though reading her thoughts, Jake handed it to her. There was reluctant admiration in his smile and something darker, more fierce. "For you."

She should have been able to control her shaking, eager hands. She should have controlled her expression of surprise and joy. But she couldn't, emotion closing her throat. "Oh," she whispered when she lifted the light tan moccasins free and ran her fingertips across the flowers on the toes.

The beaded work was exquisite, a flower accented by tiny green leaves. Cream-colored porcupine quills and rosy pink beads formed the gorgeous blossom. The leather was soft beneath her fingers. Because Jake had conspired to protect her, she shouldn't accept. Balancing the beautiful, intricately beaded moccasins against her pride took less than a heartbeat to decide. "They're beautiful. Thank you."

Jake glanced at the tiny freezer, stuffed with frozen dinners, then leaned against the counter. His gaze swept over the clutter of a fax machine and telephone, a copier and the filled bulletin board, propped against the seat. Then his gaze lowered to hers and darkened. "Making those while your bed was creaking at nights helped keep my sanity. I missed the sound last night."

The hunger in his eyes startled her before he kneeled to unlace her boots. Morganna ached to touch him, to trace that line between his brows, to smooth the shadows beneath his gleaming lashes. He slipped on the moccasins and tied the leather thongs, then held her feet in his hands, his thumbs running across the beautiful beaded blossoms. "They fit. Just like you."

Morganna walked beside him, a strong woman, confident in her skills as she pointed out her plans in the huge, looming, shadowy building. The cool wind swept through the windowless space, lifting her hair and swirling it around her. "I love working on a new project site, getting into the swing right away.... To start—a basic, balanced program, youth and adults of both sexes. Aptitude testing and teachers who recognize that a girl may want to enter the welding profession as much as a boy...woodworking, secretarial skills. There, too, it's important to remember that men are successful in those areas. I've faxed query letters to unions and various businesses to see if they'll pitch in."

Periodically Morganna drew a small tape recorder from her back pocket and noted walls, flooring and plumbing. She ordered Rita to "step on it, prioritize contacting potential builders for a meeting tomorrow morning...on the premises at eight sharp." A high-powered woman, Morganna shot out ideas, and Jake noted with interest that she had decided to warm her free hand in his back pocket. Those restless little fingers were erotic, destroying his plan to let Morganna come after him.

She shot an irritated glance up at him, then nodded at the gaping holes in the roof. "Jake. I've got this all wrong. Hiring builders is wrong...for this special project. Are there people in the community who would like to renovate this building and earn money? To demonstrate their skills and teach workers at the same time? To show a paycheck and build an investment in learning should be a plus."

He brushed aside a strand of silky black hair that webbed across her cheek. Energized by her plan, Morganna was beautiful, her green eyes sparkling. She'd brought beauty and light into his life, excitement into every second. "I'll call Hannah and Else. They can organize workers, teaching captains and learning teams."

Distracted by a mouse racing along a graffiti painted wall, Morganna shuddered and moved closer to Jake. She jerked the tape recorder up to her mouth. "Note. Tyree and his crowd are cleaning up the rubble and hauling away the junk.... Memo. Call Else and Hannah. Strike that. Call Else, she can ask Hannah.... Memo. Money makers. Media event. Charges. Celebrities from local areas.... Memo. Clothes. Jeans. No business suits."

She clicked off the recorder, jammed it into her jacket pocket and looked up at Jake. "That's it for out here. I've got a long day on the phone and setting up that first media meeting tomorrow. There's just one last memo."

"What's that?"

"This." Morganna wrapped her hands in Jake's hair and drew him down for a steamy kiss. Then she stepped back, dusted her hands lightly, tucked them in her back pockets and walked away. While Jake stared hungrily at that sway-ing, rounded backside, she grinned over her shoulder. "Memo. See yah."

Minutes later Jake jerked open the camper door a sec-ond time and stepped into the compact room. "What the hell do you mean by kissing me like that and walking off?" he demanded, nearing Morganna who had just replaced the telephone.

Nathaniel's roaring laughter sounded from the confer-ence speaker before Jake said, "I don't need an audience, Nathaniel," and punched the "off" button on the tele-phone.

"Conference call. No handset," she explained. "Okay, Jake. You're an adult. You've challenged me as a woman. It's time to titillate you."

"What?"

Morganna sighed and the sweatshirt tightened across her breasts. She bent, unlaced her boots and kicked them off and replaced them with his moccasins. "Romance you. You know the bit about the distance between sweet kisses and lovemaking. You tossed out a real challenge there, guy. I have to take you up on it. I see it as the seduction of Jake Tallman."

While he balanced his role against hers, she wiggled her toes. "Oh, I really do love these, Jake. They are beauti-ful." She studied him, then ran a fingertip across his eye-lashes. "Just like your eyes. They're liquidy, velvety and very sexy."

"What?" Jake fought the blush rising up his cheeks.

She grinned cheekily. "Memo. I'm flexible. You've made mistakes, but you're not up to my father's tactics, either. You need my protection. Oh, by the way, you're back on the baby maker list. I'd love a baby with those beautiful, ex-pressive eyes."

She flipped through her notebook and scribbled a nota-tion. "How about dinner tonight at Mamie's? My treat. I'll pick you up in my truck—" She checked her large, multi-purpose wristwatch. "Say... oh, about sixish. That should

give us an hour before the meeting at the community building."

"This won't work, Blossom," Jake said, taking a step
nearer her. He had plans of his own, and they included
tucking Morganna under *his* wing. Morganna didn't seem
to understand the proper balance of the protecting male and
the sweet, but delicate female. "You can't drive."

She tapped a pencil on the notebook and drummed her
fingers on the table. Jake's body jerked to attention; he remembered those fingers drumming low on his body.
"You're far too smug, Jake. I've been taking lessons from
Tyree. They do make automatic trucks, and Else is picking
one out for me. She's going to personally teach me how to
drive on country roads."

Else's teaching anyone to drive caused Jake to hesitate.
Then he took a step nearer, noting with satisfaction that a
shadow of uncertainty flickered in Morganna's eyes. "Tell
me that part about my seduction again. Just so I'll be able
to follow what's happening."

Her chin went up, her eyes flashing. "You'll follow. I
have a carefully planned outline. Once I have an outline, my
undertakings are always successful."

"Memo. Outline this," Jake ordered, then bent to take
her mouth. He kissed her hard, not shielding his desire.
Morganna struggled against him momentarily, then her lips
opened to his and she sank into the kiss.

Heat and hunger blended in that kiss as Morganna edged
nearer, her hands prowling through his hair, lifting it and
following the strands. Then her fingers closed hard, her
mouth slanted and she bit his lip. The nip startled him,
pushed him deeper into the kiss he'd been leashing.

Morganna's fingers ripped open his shirt, plowing
through the hair covering his chest. She shivered, her face
hot against his throat, then gently raked her nails across his
shoulder and down to his ribs. "Memo," she whispered
huskily against his jaw, then nipped it. "You held back
when we made love, Jake, dear heart, and I want it all. Being a gentleman with me won't cut it. Now that the secrets

are out of the way, I want a relationship in which we are equal partners. Think it over. Get back to me.''

Later Petey smirked. ''You been acting sulky, boss. Can't say I ever remember a woman picking you up for a date. See you at the meeting later. Else said the whole community is behind Miss Blossom. Said she's dynamite with organizing that vo-tech school. The thing is set up so that it's self-funding. Yep. Miss Blossom is one dynamite little gal, don't you think, boss?''

Jake watched the small white truck barrel down the road and skid to a stop in front of the house. The driving style smacked of Else's kamikaze techniques. Disgruntled chickens squawked and flew from the path of the truck. Pinky brayed and bucked in his pen. Black Jack reared on his back legs, showing off for his Appaloosa mares.

Dirty trotted at Morganna's heels, just like everyone else in the community, Jake noted darkly. Through the day he'd worked with Tyree and his gang to clean up the building. He'd noted that when Morganna needed his advice, she listened and weighed it carefully. She treated Tyree and his friends like valued workers, and the youths worked harder. By four o'clock the building was emptied of trash and the raunchier graffiti wire-brushed off the concrete blocks. Else had flashed Jake a grin when she visited with a huge picnic lunch of fried chicken and potato salad. ''Don't pick on Jake,'' Morganna had ordered, wiping away a grimy smudge on her cheek with the back of her hand. ''He's sweet and a bit nervous about this whole man-woman discovery thing.''

''Baby maker...Miss Blossom,'' Jake muttered, repeating the name everyone now called Morganna, as she stepped from her pickup truck. Dressed in a red sweater and matching skirt, Morganna paused on the porch, blew him a kiss through the window, then opened the door.

The knit fabric showed off every lush curve, and Jake realized he'd been holding his breath. His gaze locked to her slender legs and followed them down to her moccasins. She wiggled her toes, and his body jerked to attention. He wondered briefly if he could nibble a bit on her toes, kiss those delicate arches and work his way upward. His fingers contracted into a fist, remembering the soft juncture of her thighs.

Petey hovered around Jake, smoothing the fabric over his shoulders and plucking a wayward bit of thread from his backside. With the air of pride in his handiwork, the little cowboy patted Jake's back affectionately and ignored his glare. "Miss Blossom," Petey said in a tone dripping with gallant admiration, "come right in. Your date is ready."

She winked at Petey. "He's in a mood, isn't he?"

"Yep. A regular snit. He'll get over it, I reckon, Miss Blossom. Jake's like one of those edgy old wolves a body meets now and then. Too set in his ways and drooling at the mouth—" Petey glanced at Jake, grinned and lifted a pan of peanut butter cookies from the oven. "For the meeting, Miss Blossom. Big plans are always better met when the vittles is good desserts."

When Jake started toward Petey, Morganna stepped in front of him and raised her mouth for a kiss. Reeling in the sweet taste, Jake forgot what had angered him as Morganna snuggled in his arms.

Ten

Morganna was fully charged, electrified by her successful presentation. The community members had grasped the concept of the school, running with ideas and enthusiasm. As soon as the building committee delivered their design and material needs, she would write a fat check from Larrimore's publicity fund. Pulling strings, developing interest and plucking an educational advisors committee from thin air would be a snap. Excitement pumped through her, her energy level winging over the clouds.

She ignored the curb separating the parking lot from the highway. She also ignored Jake's succinct curse and the way his tall body tensed beneath the seat belt as her truck bumped over the six-inch curb. His hand tightened on the dashboard, but he remained silent, his lips firmly pressed together. She glanced at him when they soared beneath a streetlight. He seemed a little pale beneath the growth of beard that was darkening his jaw.

She drummed her fingers on the steering wheel and allowed the smug smile to curve her lips. She was good, re-

ally good at putting together working campaigns, and the
vo-tech school was a certainty, a prototype of its kind. Cor-
porations wanting better-trained workers nibbled eagerly at
the first crumbs of tax breaks and publicity. The campaign
launch was aggressive, complete with top media coverage
that would burst in the morning papers across the United
States. Television and radio media people had stormed her
with interviews, and blazing with success, she had tossed the
verbal ball to Jake.

Seated beside her in the pickup truck, he seemed unusu-
ally grim. In front of the television cameras, Jake could
charm candy from a baby or donations from a tight-fisted
matron. Long and lean, suited to his western shirt, jeans and
highly polished boots, Jake's image as a man dedicated to a
cause appealed to men.

She tossed her head. Committed and charming, visually
tasty or not, Jake had stepped on her wrong side.

It was a very personal slighting and one he would pay for
dearly. While she was on her high, feeding on her success,
she might as well clear up the matter of their relationship.

Everything had happened too fast, and in one short
month Jake had changed her life. She faced a full-blown
problem. She had to balance her emotions concerning Jake's
arrogance and deception—and the way his hand rode her
waist possessively in full view of the entire world. Once
during the interview—oh, she hoped they caught a good
view of her pretty new moccasins—Jake's hungry, dark-
dangerous-and-delectable male look had actually stopped
her mid-sentence.

Then he had brought her that cup of wonderful, soothing herbal tea just before the discussion of financial backing and who would expect what in return. With the Blaylock
family at his side, Jake had presented a community ready to
grow and serve educational needs for all ages. With that
strength, it was just a matter of following her plan and
wrapping up the details.

Still . . . thinking of details, there was the unresolved matter of Jake, her emotions and where things could lead.

Morganna weighed their short-term relationship. She wanted equality. Only then could she allow him to cuddle her, and she really liked that. The only way to proceed was to rip away Jake's secrets and see if their relationship to date would hold water—rather like revamping the old junction building for suitable, long-term use. Or refashioning her business wardrobe to include bosom-exposing date dresses.

Jake braced his long legs against the floorboard as she skidded to a stop in front of her camper. "I just want to check my messages before taking you home, Jake. I'll be right back."

His hand wrapped around hers as she inserted the key into the camper door. "Let me."

"Oh, right. Fine." The issue wasn't the war, and Morganna decided to let him play the gentleman as long as he could. When she popped some of her discoveries in his face, she would enjoy the veneer slipping.

She stepped back, surprised when Jake went into the dark camper first. He flipped on the lights and quickly scanned the empty bedroom and bathroom as she entered.

He opened the refrigerator door, slid his hand beneath the table and cabinets, lifted curtains and blinds away and generally checked every nook. "I've seen this technique used in detective stories," Morganna stated, her temper catching little sparks. "There's no need for this."

Jake continued to search. "Surely you don't think that Ames has the nerve to doing anything so rash...Jake?" she prompted when he jerked apart the bed she had made perfectly. It had taken her eight tries to get those sheets wrinkle free. "Jake, stop it."

"Make me," he returned easily, his dark eyes flashing, running down her body hungrily. "Who's great idea was national media coverage at this stage?" he demanded.

She tilted her head, angling her jaw. "Media is a necessary element on a project of this nature. I know my business."

"Uh-huh," Jake agreed without commitment. He ran his fingers through his hair, rubbed the back of his neck and closed his eyes briefly.

He looked so harried, so torn that Morganna's anger slid away and she stepped closer. She lifted on tiptoe for a light kiss and patted that taut muscle contracting in his cheek. "Jake, I'm perfectly capable of taking care of myself. I've done it for years."

His warm lips pressed against her palm, his expressive eyes darkening with concern. When his head bent, Morganna raised to meet his kiss. It was sweet and tender—

The blow against the side of the camper unbalanced them. Jake braced a hand against the wall and wrapped her to his body with the other. Then a motor revved, and the second blow tilted the camper, crashing against the metal siding and frame. Jake landed on the bed, breaking Morganna's fall. The next instant the vehicle rammed again then sped off into the night.

Jake's fingers clamped around her wrist, drawing her after him and into her truck. "Watch their lights," he ordered, pushing the driver's seat back for his longer legs. He snapped her seat belt into place, then his own. "Hold on."

The vehicle rounded a small hill and disappeared. Jake drove Morganna's pickup toward a small dirt lane, then soared across the bumps. He eased it through a trickling creek and up a rock embankment. At the crest of a stump-covered hill, he asked, "See anything? There are four roads down there, all leading into timber trails."

When she shook her head, unable to speak after the frightening ride upward, Jake eased the truck down the hill. He scraped the bottom several times and narrowly missed a deer blinded by the headlights. He parked at an intersection, scanning the roads. "See anything?" he asked again.

"Nothing. But you've muddied my truck and dented a perfectly good, brand new fender over nothing. This incident is probably some disgruntled inebriant wanting his junction retreat returned. No doubt a territorial male. A ritualistic last stand."

Jake looked at her blankly for a moment, then swore.

She crossed her arms over her chest and settled back in the seat. "Now get us out of here. There are a few matters we need to discuss and now isn't the time or place. I need a bit of rest before dealing with your high-handed tactics. I'll drop you off and see you tomorrow."

Jake closed his eyes, gripped the steering wheel and shook his head. "Are you muttering, Jake?" she asked, miffed at his reaction to losing whomever in the night.

He acted so bruised, so dark and brooding, but Morganna decided he wasn't going to spoil her plans for the night. She intended to deposit Jake on his doorstep with a good-night kiss. While she could allow some plans to run awry, others had to remain firmly locked in place.

Later Morganna was so busy kissing Jake good-night that she didn't notice he had eased her inside the house.

Jake's hard, hungry mouth was just the topper she needed after flying high on her success.

Though his mouth was the only contact, Jake managed to nibble, caress, nuzzle and tempt her over his doorstep.

The slight, metallic click chipped away at her concentration. Jake's tempting mouth continued to brush hers. "What was that?" she asked huskily, unwilling to open her eyes.

"Mmm? The lock." His warm mouth drifted across her cheek, his teeth tugging at her earlobe.

Easing back slightly, Morganna found her hips against Jake's kitchen counter. She opened her eyes to his black, gleaming ones. There was just that whimsical curve to his mouth, a tiny dimple toying in his dark cheek while he waited for her response. If only that strand of glossy black hair wasn't crossing his brow... if only he didn't look so tempting, she thought desperately.

Jake reached past her to jerk open the kitchen window. "Petey!"

"Yeah, boss! I wired a buzzer to the house in case I spot anything."

"Oh, great. The fort is safe," Morganna mumbled, trying to ease away from Jake. He moved closer, his heat and scent swirling around her. Pushing against him was like pushing against a stone statue. Her fingers tapped his chest. A warm, rippling, devastating male without the fig leaf. He eased closer, and she shivered, aware of the hunter's gleam in his eyes.

"You're a success, Blossom. So you decided to make a big splash and invite the media?" Jake asked as his hands slid slowly, firmly to her hips and locked there.

Morganna frowned. Jake tugged her against his hips, inserted his thigh between hers and nudged her rhythmically. She tried to concentrate, focusing away from excitement heating her. Her body responded instantly, a liquid burst of heat from the core of her being. He frightened her a bit, the tension running through him setting off tiny pings inside her. She rested her hands on his wrists, looking up at him. "They're putting together a documentary on how small, rural communities can offer advantages to their youth and to people who need to be retrained for jobs. Tonight was the first in a series in the progress of the school."

Jake's fingers opened, spanning her hips possessively. "A media blitz will draw Ames like a hungry coyote. That is why you're staying here with me tonight. Your camper is unsafe."

Morganna placed her hands on his chest, pushing slightly against the rippling muscle beneath his cotton dress shirt. Jake's jaw hardened. He inhaled, stepping back slightly to allow her to move away. "I want you with me," he said quietly. "Stay with me."

She shot a suspicious glance at him. Jake stood apart, his head lifted arrogantly, but something wary and vulnerable shimmered behind those long lashes. His long fingers trembled, straightened, pushed against his thighs, then formed fists. She ached for his pain, for his scars and knew that he had not asked lightly. "Well, maybe we could chat about it..." she offered airily and found herself being scooped off her feet.

Jake entered the bedroom and tossed her to his bed with a curt order. "Stay put."

Morganna landed on her back and found Jake's weight pinning her down. She squirmed a bit, found it useless and glared up at him.

His smile devastated her. Laughter sparkled beneath his lashes, his grin boyish and dashing.

Thoughts of little black-haired, sparkling-eyed, beautiful children cluttered her decision to fight him too hard. The children danced around in her brain with thoughts of Jake in her life, filling her nights. While she fought the images of the children and perhaps a baby resting snugly in the walnut cradle, Jake's arousing body was clearly at hand.

"Titillate me," he ordered, his grin widening.

"Not a chance. You acted like a macho cowboy out on a bloody manhunt earlier, and from now on I'm calling the shots." Was that her voice? The sexy, inviting tone startled her. She squirmed a bit for effect. Though she really didn't want to leave the heavy warm weight of Jake's body, she couldn't give in that easily.

"You were. But you're in my bed now," Jake challenged, bending to nuzzle her throat. "Rules change. Home rules win."

Darn, there goes that one, she thought. Her treacherous body was already weakening, moistening, aching for his. She drummed her fingers on his shoulders. "Your boots are on," she said to distract him. She really wanted to get the upper hand in this situation, and it was difficult to do with Jake's tempting mouth so near.

"Mmm? So they are."

"You can't have things all your way."

"I agree."

"Now isn't a good time to challenge me, Jake," she warned, just as Jake's tongue found her ear. A hungry shiver went spiraling down her body. "I've just had a successful presentation, and my energy level is high, despite your little race through the wilderness. After other victories, I've spent hours in my private workout room. Trust me.

I feel like I could leap from mountain top to mountain top right now. I warn you, now is no time to start anything—"

Her words were muffled beneath the sweater that Jake had been tugging steadily upward. He tossed it aside and cradled her jaw in his hand. "Okay, fireball." His drawl was slow, soft and thrilling. "You're making an important difference. I'm proud of you. The education you're providing will change lives. Just as you've changed mine.... I didn't want to care, didn't want to have another woman in my heart," he whispered slowly. "But you're here now. Will you stay with me?"

He spread his hand over her breast, claiming it gently. The gesture took her breath away. This beautiful man wanted her, wanted what she was and waited for her answer.

Still. Pride demanded that she have her due. She cleared her throat and tried to ignore the warm finger slowly stroking her mouth. "Uh...let me get this straight. We've known each other a month...." She stopped to suck the finger tempting her lips and instantly Jake inhaled.

She liked that. She really liked the way he responded to her. For good measure she bit his fingertip and watched his beautiful eyes darken. "You're working under some misguided apprehension that I need protection—"

"I need you in my life," he whispered slowly, spacing each word.

A tremor of delight swept over her. "You can't have things all your way. Though I did appreciate how you backed me tonight, offering to work with Larrimore's every step of the way." Jake's hand had stayed at her waist during the presentation. The courtly gesture was inappropriate in the boardroom or during business hours. But it appealed immensely to her, then and now.

She eased off the bed, allowing herself space to think, and Jake followed. Morganna smoothed her clothing, glanced at Jake and wondered about the passion she sensed running beneath his taut expression. There was more there, too. A man with strength and ideals, a man who wanted her and could withstand her energies—

In the dimly lit room, Jake jerked off his boots and plopped one on the floor, then the other, on his way toward her. Morganna glanced at those boots and couldn't remember a time when they weren't polished and neatly placed together. Their tussle had mussed Jake's gleaming black hair, and he shoved his fingers through it, his eyes wary as he took another step toward her.

Morganna's back touched the wall, and Jake placed his hands on either side of her head. "Well?" he asked, sliding a finger beneath the strap of her lacy peach bra.

"Well?" she returned challengingly. "If you hold back this time, Jake, I'll never forgive you," she whispered shakily.

The moonlight skimmed through the window, slanting a silvery strip across Jake's mouth. It moved slightly, his voice dark and rasping in the silence broken only by the beating of her heart. "Come with me," he said simply.

With one jerk of his finger Jake broke the fragile strap, then traced a line across the rounded tops of her breasts to the other strap. It snapped easily.

Taking her time, meeting his challenging gaze, Morganna slid her hands to his shirt. The pearl snaps tore open easily, and she pushed aside the fabric to rest her parted mouth on his warm skin.

Jake's heart beat rapidly, pounding against her lips. There was power there, passion running high for her, and something deeper, something sacred and pure. Commitments of bodies, of minds and lives wove through the moonlit air, magically drawing them nearer.

In one sweep he stripped away her clothing and stood back, his legs spread, daring her to meet him.

Morganna stepped nearer his challenge, her trembling hands unable to unbuckle his belt. Impatiently Jake completed the task, stepping free of his clothing.

She touched the hard angular planes of his body in wonder. His long, artistic fingers smoothed her shoulders, her breasts, sliding lower to curve possessively around the roundness of her hips. His head angled arrogantly above her, challenging her, as his fingertips pressed gently into her breasts, then lower. They glided across her stomach, pressing against her intimately before entering.

Trembling, fighting to stand, Morganna allowed Jake's fingers to enter her body. This was his ceremony, a claiming without words, and she wanted this desperately. Bracing her hands on his shoulders, Morganna rode the tiny contractions already beginning. "You're staying," Jake said quietly.

"Yes." She moved against him, stood with her breasts touching him.

"Yes," he whispered again, picking her up and carrying her to his bed.

Jake entered her smoothly, his mouth taking hers the instant they fell to the bed. His hands swept over her, touching, finding, lifting her higher. When his mouth heated her throat, her breasts, Morganna cried out with passion, cried out in the age-old magic that drove him harder, deeper.

His heart raced against hers, his fingers sliding between hers, securing them against the bed. Fire and pleasure danced along their bodies, shooting higher. She met his kiss fiercely, taking, giving, draining.

She cried out again, the ripples of pleasure beginning deep within her, growing, echoing.... Jake's hard thighs moved within hers, his lips moving, whispering against her cheek, urging her higher. She moved aside, and he followed, kissing away the tears on her hot skin.

They were one, their souls flying, igniting, dancing across time. Jake demanded more, fiercely taking, yet taking no more than she gave.

Morganna caught him close, snaring him in a sweet tangle of arms and legs, drawing them nearer the fire. "Oh, no, you don't, Jake," she whispered when he lifted his weight slightly away, his fingers trembling around her wrist. "Don't you dare back away now. I won't settle for less than everything."

He shuddered, hesitated, then moved back near the fire, demanding, hunting, taking. Moving above her, his features taut with passion, Jake bent to kiss her. A fierce warrior taking what he wanted, making love without restraint, matching her passion with his; Jake's heart became hers and she tasted his soul with a cry.

Lifting to meet him, Morganna kissed him hard, meeting his lips and his tongue, slanting her mouth against his, urging, tempting.

They flew higher, unwilling to relinquish the pleasure, straining against the ultimate. Then Jake cried out her name and she his, and they fell slowly into a satiny mist.

Jake rested on her heavily, and Morganna stroked his back, savoring the moment. On the pillow his head turned to her throat, his kisses hard and quick. Against her breast, his heart thudded unevenly, slowing. Then Jake nipped her shoulder, his body pushing hungrily down on hers.

She understood. The night was for them, for bonding of lives, of bodies. Neither would forget the storm, nor what it meant. There would be no turning back, the commitment made.

Their eyes met and locked, understanding, promising. In the silence of the moonlight, Jake asked again, his body trembling against hers. "Yes," she whispered again. "Yes."

Jake's hunger the second time was no less fierce than the first, and Morganna cried out, shattered by the beauty of what they had created.

He gently roused her again during the night, then despite her grumbles, showered with her and tucked her back in bed. Jake cuddled her close, his long fingers closing possessively around one breast.

Jake awoke to Morganna straddling his hips, shaking him awake, her expression fierce. She covered her body with a pillow. "Jake, wake up. I'm not finished with our discussion yet."

He blinked, aware that he was already aroused and cradled between Morganna's warm thighs. He found the line of her hip and followed it to her rounded bottom, cupping it. Morganna reached to plump the pillow behind his head, and he kissed the tip of her breast. "Stop that." Then she trembled, her palms smoothing his chest. "Jake. This is important. You will never, never place me aside in one of those containers of yours—"

He frowned. "Containers?"

"You have a nasty little habit of placing the things you love inside baskets or trunks. A sort of out of sight, out of mind thing with you. You've hidden yourself and you've hidden the things that are a part of you. I suspect you're hiding a great deal more, like a real knack for colors and textures." She hit his chest. "I won't be parceled out into a neat little carton of your life, do you hear me?" she demanded, shaking his shoulders.

Jake fought the laughter bubbling in him, fought it erupting and spilling into the two o'clock hour. The chuckle began and a second one followed. "Jake?" Morganna asked softly. "This isn't a laughing matter. It's important that all the criteria for our relationship are aboveboard, explained to a T. You've got to take me seriously or the relationship is off."

He shifted under her weight, adjusted it carefully and ran the flat of his hand from her pale shoulder down to her thighs. "I take you very seriously."

"This basket thing, Jake," she prodded. "I've noticed that you neatly pack away everything. I can't allow that to happen to me...." In the moonlight Morganna bit her lip and averted her hot face.

Jake stroked her cheek, lifting her chin with his finger. "It won't."

She inhaled as though she had been holding her breath. "Good. I just wanted to see if we agreed on the ground rules. I wouldn't want any misrepresentation after what we just...what we just...what just transpired between us."

He toyed with a silky strand of hair. "When we made love? When you cried out how much you wanted me?"

She flushed and swallowed, shivering beneath his caress. "Would it please you, Blossom, if I opened...spread my life before you?"

She cleared her throat. "Yes, I would like that very much. Start with this—" She tossed an audio tape to his chest. "The name is 'Jake's Song.' That's you, isn't it?"

Jake sat up slowly, easing from beneath her and carrying the tape into the living room. Draped in a sheet, Morganna followed and settled on the couch while Jake bent to start a fire. He was beautiful; broad shoulders and hard haunches flowed into long, muscled legs. "The music is old, very old, passed down from my father and his father before him."

He shrugged, watching the firelight, which cast flickering strips across his face. "When I knew I would not have children, I wanted the music to continue. I wanted children to know what was in their soul. A friend connected me with a school for sightless children. They 'see' my carved animals through their hands, and for a time I have my children and tell my stories as my father did before me." Jake struggled with his past, fighting the darkness, and stilled when a warm tear slid down his shoulder.

Morganna's pale fingers lightly smoothed his chest, and he brushed away her tears with his lips. He eased her to his lap, then leaned back against the couch and settled down to hold her for a lifetime. Her arms cradled him, sheltered him from the cold, the pain. She stroked his hair, gently easing away the shadowy past. Morganna's head rested against his shoulder, her eyes wide in the shadows. "What am I, Jake? Where am I in your life?"

He closed his eyes, willing the words to flow from him, to open his scarred heart. Pain fluttered in him, tearing and soaring away like a bird released to freedom. With care Jake placed his hand on her breast and lower, more intimately on her body. "You are wind in the sunlight, stirring the colors in my heart. When I am with you, in you, life begins again," he whispered simply. "It is warm in your body, tight with honey, and then I find my heart. It hurts at first, tearing. Then in you, with you, the wind sweeps over me, making me new. The air is sweet with your scent, and you flow over me . . . I forget what was and seek what can be—"

Jake stroked her breast, tracing the shape. "Yet there is more. When you smile, my mind stops. When you laugh, there is music." He nuzzled her hair, gathering her closer in a strong cradle of arms and legs. "Then the scent and the dreams.... There is more.... I am the hunter, stalking you for the joy of living. You run, you turn. Each look enchants, completes what is in my soul. I will keep your picture in my heart forever."

Her hands covered his, slender, delicate power warming his skin. She eased higher slightly, turning her lips to his cheek and tasting his tears with her tongue. "Yes, there is more."

Hours later, Morganna refused to answer the telephone, snuggling closer to Jake's hard warm body. He shifted slightly and she followed, settling her cheek over the even beating of his heart. "Yes," Jake's voice was husky with sleep and something else, she noted smugly. Sleeping à la nude with Jake had advantages. He stopped her wandering fingers, raising them to his mouth and nibbling the tips. "Yes, Nathaniel. She's safe. Yes, I'm keeping a close eye on her. Yes, the trailer was damaged, and I'm not letting her stay the night there...."

Her father's voice roared over the lines, threatening torture dungeons to anyone who harmed his little girl. Jake's lips slowly curved into a smile, his hand stroking her bare hip. When he replaced the telephone to its cradle, Jake lay over Morganna's body in a quick, lithe motion. "He'll be here in two days. Has to clear up a bit of business. Paul will be here in the morning."

He grinned and bent to gently nuzzle her throat with his stubbled jaw. When she giggled, squirming beneath him, Jake laughed outright. Then the mood changed, stilled, and stretched into a long, magical moment before the storms took them again.

Jake awoke suddenly, startled by the hard plop to his stomach. A huge frog stared at him, while in the kitchen, a youth exclaimed, "Morganna Larrimore. You slept until ten o'clock in the morning. The world is turning over. Look at you, you actually yawned...*at ten o'clock in the morning*. What's that on your throat? Oh...my...gosh! It looks...like some guy with a beard got ver-ry close.''

''Well! You don't have to act as if it is an impossibility,'' Morganna stated huffily. ''After all, I am a woman.''

''I forget. I guess I think of you as more generic. You've never done this before. Are you a closet wanton?'' he asked with interest. ''My sis, actually passionate about something other than business and causes? Hey, the world has stopped spinning on its axis.... Ouch, that hurt.''

Jake lifted the frog aside and slipped on his jeans as the discussion continued. ''Morganna Fay Larrimore. Pops will turn righteous. Rita is barely holding him down now to complete a merger. He's all stoked up to build that school and raging over some guy named Ames. Who is this lovemaking dude, anyway? One of those stuffed shirts you've been picking over for husband material? Nah, couldn't be. Who? Man, what a mystery.''

Jake tossed the frog to the youth, whose eyes widened then jerked to Morganna who stood huddled in Jake's flannel shirt, her long legs gleaming in the bright morning sun. She looked rumpled and cuddly and uncertain, though she scowled at Jake. ''Oh, great. You couldn't wait for a few minutes. This is my brother, Paul...Jake Tallman.''

''It is my house. Unless you want me to vacate.'' Jake shook the youth's hand, recognizing Morganna's fair skin and sleek black hair in his features. There the resemblance stopped. Tall and thin, Paul wore thin-rimmed glasses, a saggy sweater and loose, knee-length shorts. His heavy-duty joggers were topped by neon orange socks.

The youth studied Jake while he made coffee. Morganna jumped behind Jake when Petey strolled through the slightly opened kitchen door with a bucket of milk. ''Figured since the door was finally opened and there's a van out front, it was safe enough to come in. I stayed up most of the night, on the lookout. Been thinking this milk would sour before you decided to wake up.''

Petey stared at Paul, then at the huge frog who hopped onto his boot. "Vittles," he said simply. "Ain't had frog legs in a long time." He glanced at Morganna, who was blushing behind Jake's shoulder. "You look real pretty, Miss Blossom."

"She does that." Jake eased back slightly, and Morganna's breasts warmed his skin.

"Jake, this is horrible. Get them out of here," she whispered, her hands were locked to his waist. "Do something. Explain—"

"Can't. It would be impolite." He liked having the house full, Morganna warming his back.

"Oh!" Her fingers pinched his backside and Jake trapped her wrists, bringing her arms around him. When she lifted her mouth to protest, he turned his head and kissed her. Her lips pushed gently into his and sunlight danced in his heart.

"I owe you," she promised darkly, but her arms held him tighter.

Paul stared down at the milk. "Man. Real country milk. Makes the best butter. Put it on sourdough pancakes and you've got a feast. Want me to cook?" He jerked open the stove, looked into the oven and jerked out a skillet. "Man, oh, man. Real cast iron stuff and a gas cooking stove."

A truck rumbled, then died in front of the house. Tyree stepped into the open doorway a second later. "Whoa. That has got to be the biggest frog ever."

"Mine, dude," Paul said, admiring Petey's sourdough starter. "His name is Sheik. He's on rest and relaxation before we start training for the next match. Dad's bad vibes, the way he raked me over the coals before the last match, affected Sheik's karma."

"Oh, well. Oh, well," Morganna said airily. "Let's have a convention right here, right now. Let's make butter and pancakes and talk about jumping frogs. Go right ahead without me."

"Man, this is one piece of jumbo jumper," Tyree noted appreciatively, cuddling the frog and dismissing the simmering woman.

The bathroom door slammed behind Morganna. "Hey, Sis. Just be glad Dad's not here. He can be a demon on this righteous stuff," Paul called out.

"Boss, you need to build on," Petey stated with a grin, just as Dirty strolled into the kitchen and plopped his bottom on a rug. Curds sashayed in front of him, her tail high. "Reckon your hideout has been invaded."

Jake couldn't stop the happy grin lurking around his lips.

Eleven

The second week of June Jake returned wearily from a long night of repairing fences and reclaiming wandering cattle to find Morganna's curt note. The pink dawn slid into the window and Jake's fear rose, suffocating him. A glance told him that she had taken her belongings, cleaned his house of paper clutter, dried lily of the valley and daffodil bouquets and the basket of quilt pieces.

The night's chill clung to the house as Jake slowly pushed open the door to their bedroom. The bed was neatly made, the frothy bits of lace that usually clung to doorknobs and bedposts gone.

Jake gripped the note, crushing it in his fingers and fighting the pain.

He forced himself to breathe, to carefully remove his gloves with trembling fingers, then rip open the note.

The school is a reality. I'll tidy up the project and you'll have the paperwork within the week. Hannah and Else have a good grasp on the project, and I'll be in touch with them about details. Ames died four months ago. My father set up the whole thing. I am sorry you were trapped in his plans. Don't call. M.

Also enclosed was a sheriff's report. The truck that bashed Morganna's camper had been rented to one Nathaniel Larrimore.

"'Tidy up the project,'" Jake repeated slowly, before he picked up the telephone to dial Nathaniel's number. Tidying up loose ends might be a Larrimore trait, but Jake had plans of his own. They included Morganna in his life— however and whenever he could have her. He wouldn't allow her pride to keep them apart.

Nathaniel's sleepy voice answered. "Jake? Yes, she's back in the office. Furious with me. Raging through workloads like a powerhouse. She's back to being a workaholic, twice over. Uh...uh...let me call you back in a minute, okay? I worked on a little project last night and have to clear it away. Be just a minute."

When he called back, his voice was irritated. "Women. They're not logical. Rita took offense when I said she was a project that needing clearing away. Okay, I suppose you're calling about Morganna. She's left strict orders that she isn't receiving your calls. She told me to butt out."

Jake eased a flannel shirt that was hanging on the bedroom doorknob to his face. Her scent clung to it, and a fist slammed into his stomach, reminding him of the loneliness before Morganna entered his life. "She's an emotional woman."

"Hell of a business mind. A regular powerhouse and she's mad this time. Really mad. Some sort of injured female sensibility, I guess. Women's minds are quirky at best.... Damn. Rita and I were getting along fine until I termed her 'a project.' She's a real woman, everything a man could want. I'm going to marry her.... She acted like a mad hen. Now why would she act like that?"

Jake had his own problems with one very special woman and the future he wanted with her. At the moment that future was sinking slowly. Morganna was a proud woman, and her dignity must have taken a bashing when she discovered Nathaniel's deceit. He had an idea that Nathaniel didn't understand the bruised egos of Rita or his daughter. "What happened?"

"Who knows. Rita hasn't been happy about this whole thing with Morganna. She considers it a deception."

Jake was quickly losing patience. "Nathaniel."

"Okay. I'm guilty. Ames died four months ago, plowed his sportscar into the back end of a truck going west. Of course I didn't know that then . . . Rita had been dropping tidbits about Ames being a dangerous man and I found a threatening note in one of my daughter's files. Only after I put a team on it did I discover that Rita was behind the whole smoke screen. She knew that Ames was dead and that I'd maneuver Morganna out of the way once I scented danger—smart woman, Rita. She knew I was mad as all get out. The idea that Morganna was in danger overrode everything else. But something had to be done about Ames. The situation was critical and I had to get my daughter out of the office. I had to reel her in slowly. Challenge the hell out of her before she took off— How the hell would I know she'd choose the top of a killer mountain?" Nathaniel asked, frustrated.

"So Rita led a merry paperwork chase, and you backed into the camper. Hit it a little hard, didn't you?" Jake asked, suspecting that Morganna's pride was injured and that she probably viewed him as an accomplice.

"Clutch. Haven't used a truck in years. That clunker grabbed gears too quick," Nathaniel muttered warily. "Okay. The reason Rita thought that she had to get my daughter out of the office. . . . I found a list, titled "Baby-Makers" on the back of her memo to me. Under it was another list called "Potential Marriage." Recognized every man's name. Not a one could hold my daughter in line. Then I started thinking about being a grandfather and who would be sitting across the Thanksgiving and Christmas dinner table from now on. Bartonwick headed the list—

smells like mouthwash and parts his hair in the middle. Wears those squinty little glasses and bow ties. He's a dead bore. I don't think the man ever blinks. I kept seeing miniature Bartonwicks lined up across from the Christmas turkey and I went berserk.''

Nathaniel breathed heavily. "I guess that's when Rita figured she'd better step in and set up the little deception about Ames. I managed to challenge my daughter, and she took off for that damned mountain. She needed rescuing and the pilot said it wasn't safe to go in. Then I thought of you. After that the scam fell smoothly into place. You're a whole lot better alternative than Bartonwick, Jake."

Jake tightened his lips. He had plans for Thanksgivings and Christmases with Morganna and none of them included Bartonwick children. "Thanks. And Nathaniel?"

"Yeah?"

"Butt out."

Else and Hannah took the reins of the project, slipping him update tidbits about Morganna, who was "tidying up business ends." Jake had his own tidying to do, and it meant cleaning out the stormy corners of his life. With time, and the new paints and stiff brushes, he would open his heart to Morganna, show her what he was, what was in his heart. She had opened that frightening doorway, and he would step through it.

Scraped away by his parents' death, locked in the shadows by the taunting of one brutal foster parent and teenage toughs, his skills were rusty, fighting his hands and his mind. He'd survived by pushing them away, closing his heart and emotions to the brutal torments. As Morganna would not be placed neatly aside in his heart, nor would his talents. The two, the woman and the need to create, to blend colors and textures, twined around each other.

His mind was restless, furious to create, to tell the woman how he loved, who he was deep inside, beneath the scars. Then the images began to respond, the brushes sweeping freely over the canvas, filling his days and midnight hours.

Colors merged, blended, flowed in mauve, tans and creams. Jake blended darker tans, fighting desperately, pushing himself and his art too quickly, impatiently. Then Morganna lay across the canvas, her pale shoulder smooth within the mauve and cream tints, her eyes beckoning seductively, her hair lying as though it had left a lover's demanding fingers. When he crated the large canvas and sent it to Morganna, he sent a bit of his heart, aching for her.

He rested for a day, lying stripped of his clothing in the sunlit meadow, feeling the elements swirl around him, sensing his life spreading out, absorbing, taking images and scents into his mind, storing them. He had always seen the beauty, felt it waiting in him, and now it spilled into his hands.

He wanted Morganna, willed her to know by his canvas how much he needed her to survive. Fear and pain drove him, pushed him past his limits as he stepped into the shadows. Giving into his talent, remembering the flow of his father's hands shaping pottery, his mother's weaving and making dyes from plants and clay, Jake remembered how his father's eyes gleamed when he told of his courting time.

Finding his stride with a second painting, Jake caught Morganna as she had held the child, the tender smile lurking around her mouth, the tilt of her head to the baby's.

Slowly the elements that he had pushed back throughout his life came back, running true and strong. Time stretched back and to the future, weaving his ancestry, his parents around him. Blending the wilderness and his essence deep within him.

But she was there, too. The woman. With mysterious eyes the shade of dark green leaves in sultry summer heat. With a smile that sent his heart soaring strong like an eagle or quivering softly like a newborn rabbit sheltering in its nest, fearing what lay in the sunshine and the wind.

All this Jake consumed, storing his emotions, his senses, and blending them with the need of his love.

The ritual dance of his courtship was timeless, and Jake revered the custom, drawing it from his childhood memories. If she allowed him to take her this time, she would not leave him again. Morganna had not sent back his offerings, and his bridal offering had been accepted. When the time was right, he would go for her. In his way. Just as his father had done and his father before him.

The Blaylocks dropped in, helped Petey with the ranch work and generally gave Jake his most precious gift, that of time to develop his talent. His journey was painful, and they understood his need to heal and grow, meeting the future.

Nathaniel called the first week of July. "Jake. I didn't know you could draw. I always thought of you as . . . well, tough, the ultimate cowboy, needing no one. This drawing stuff is damned sensitive stuff. The picture of Morganna with a kid is great, ah . . . but the other . . . It's unnerving, gives the impression that she's nude with that one bare shoulder. She hung it over the boardroom table. Thought it would brighten up a dark spot in the room or something. My daughter is not, nor never has been . . . uh . . . seductive as you have painted her. She's steaming on that damn canvas, Jake. Steaming," Nathaniel's voice rose an indignant notch, then lowered. "Uh . . . maybe you could ask for it back?"

"How's Rita?" Jake asked to distract Nathaniel. His thoughts skimmed to future paintings of Morganna. It pleased him that Morganna displayed his gift, a good sign. *Or she could refuse.* Colors, whites and blacks, circled him, swirling, the colors of cold, stark fear.

"Rita?" Nathaniel's voice softened, then announced cheerfully. "I'm going to be a father again. Now there's a steamy woman. We got married two weeks ago and she's sick in the mornings already. I love this woman, Jake. Sorry, but I've got my hands full here. Planning to spend more time at home and tidying up ends so Morganna won't run wild with power the moment my back is turned. You're on your own. Sorry about leaving you out on a limb, but Rita—ah, Rita needs me. What a woman. By the way, Jake. You sound bone tired, better get some rest."

Jake relaxed slightly. With Nathaniel hopping around Rita, that left little time for him to insert his custom-made,

Italian loafers into the future that Jake planned with Morganna. It was all a matter of details, moving slowly, step by step and tidying up those loose little ends. Like proving that he loved her and that she was his soul, his life.

Jake checked into the progress of the school regularly. His tape distributor in New Mexico offered to contribute sales of any music and stories that Jake wanted to create. Tyree visited one morning, strolled through Jake's home and stood in front of his latest canvas, a picture of a boy, lying on his back and playing a flute in a flower-filled meadow. "I'm going back to high school," Tyree announced slowly. "I want to teach at the vo-tech school and Paul said I should get more education. So I am. Paul has a master's degree and wants to teach something, too. He says he's a nurturing soul and that business is wrong for him. His old man exploded and his sister pulled something called a 'checkmate.' Anyway, she blocked his dad's power play to get Paul on what he called 'back on track'. Funny, I never thought about Morg being all that tough. She always seemed sort of cute and fuzzy, cuddly, you know?"

Jake pushed away the smile teasing his lips. He knew just how cuddly Morganna could be and how badly he wanted her back in his arms. He gave her his soul on each canvas. His heart on each song.

There was the hunter in him, too. The dark primitive nature driven by his fiery passions and the woman who could match them.

Dressed in scarlet running shorts, Morganna found her stride, gliding over the Kansas City streets in the late July morning. She sweated, heart beating, fighting to push the restless empty night away. Lungs aching, her bare legs swished through the cool air that would bake the city later. She circled a paperboy, a baker carrying his goods to a café and swooped through a small park, acknowledging a policeman's wave with her nod.

She grimly pushed her body, fighting memories of Jake, dreaming of him, wishing for him. She forced her mind to the current merger's details, itemizing, clarifying—

Jake. She saw him rising above her, dark and straining with passion. Saw that devastating white gleam of teeth in the dark, rugged planes of his face. His eyes shot out thunderbolts, and heat shot along her body.

The details of the workman's health plans were fuzzy, needing revamping—

Jake. He had stirred passion in her, and it simmered all night, every night and periodically throughout her business conferences.

Jake. His beautiful paintings caused her to cry. Surely she wasn't the mysterious siren on his first picture, despite the distinctive shape of her eyes and light coloring. The cut and color of her hair was similar, yet the sleek disarray suggested that the subject was reclining in bed....

Her smile was more of a glow in the painting of her and the child. That dark-haired Blaylock baby. Morganna remembered the gentle way Jake had introduced her to love and ran faster.

She blew a drop of sweat away from her cheek, breathing hard, her heart pumping furiously.The day loomed before her, chockful with appointments and paperwork. She dipped under an awning that was just being lifted for the day, leapt over a bundle of newspapers, ran another block and swung into Larrimore's parking lot.

If the prework conference for the new mall went well in the morning, she should have time to add the sky blue pieces of Hannah's baby's gown to her quilt before dinner.

Cooling down, she circled the lot twice and surged up the stairs rather than taking the elevator. Her new secretary's brand-new business look was frazzled around the edges. She wrung her hands as Morganna jogged in place. "Ms. Larrimore. There's a man in your office. There's a helicopter on the roof. He's a cowboy. He's terribly good-looking—"

Morganna ripped open her door, charged through it and hit Jake's chest.

His arms wrapped around her immediately, the force of her body taking his back to the wall. Morganna shook free instantly, jerking her damp headband off and tossed it to her desk. She parted her mouth to scold him and blinked at Jake's wide grin.

"Your instructions said not to call. I didn't," he reminded her, taking in her vivid red, sweaty top and running shorts.

She shivered beneath that hot, passionate sweep of black eyes. Wearing faded jeans, his polished Sunday boots, a cream-colored western shirt rolled up at the forearms and a devastating grin, Jake caused her heart to stop. There was an edge to him, a taut, daring, challenging aura—his eyes glinted with it.

Jake's hair was longer, and there was a tiny, fresh cut along his jaw. He had lost weight. Dark circles rested beneath his eyes. His eyes—she studied that glint, the predatory light that had fastened intently on her. Why, he had the look of a hunter.

She fought the happy surge of her heart, fought throwing herself into his arms. She had to tend her pride after all. She lifted her chin, grabbed the quilt he had been holding and tossed it to her desk. "Why are you here? And what do you mean sending me those beautiful pictures and lovely taped songs?"

They were beautiful songs, filled with sunlight and wind and cool, hazy summer days. Morganna swallowed, moistening her dry throat. She'd cried for hours, wrapping Jake's shirt around her and holding her lovely moccasins tightly, while the flute music curled through her heart.

"My father and his father before him sent a gift to their wives—the bridal price," Jake stated slowly, his voice running deep with emotion. His hand opened, caressed the smooth sweep of her hair slowly. He slid a finger through the silky texture, lifted one strand and studied the gleaming lights as it slid away.

"The bridal price—as in marriage?" Morganna asked, her heart beating wildly. Jake took a step and Morganna eased back, her eyes widening as he leaned over her, placing his hands on the desk. His scent swirled around her, and the gleam in his eyes dried her throat. "Be careful, Jake. I'm always energized after a run. Lots of oxygen in the blood after exercise, you know."

"How's the baby maker list going?" he asked, watching her intently from the shadows of those long lashes. His fingers wrapped around her wrist, caressing the smooth inner skin.

There was a feeling of heat, of pleasure, of claiming in his long fingers. The gentle strength would last beyond forever.

"Oh . . . fair," she answered as he bent to lick a drop of sweat from between her breasts. The caress caused her to shiver.

Jake's hard mouth curved sensuously. "I love you, Blossom," he whispered slowly, huskily. "Marry me."

She blinked, wondering distantly if her night dreams of Jake had shifted into her days. Maybe the sleepless nights were catching up to her—

"Oh…oh, I couldn't…much too busy today." She closed her eyes, struggling against her pride. Jake's hand ran down her body, skimming it. His fingers slid between her legs, pressing against her gently, firmly, then slid higher to cup her breast. He bent to kiss it reverently.

The intimate, primitive claiming startled her. *The bridal price,* he had said.

When Jake lifted his head, she saw hunger and emotions that would last throughout their lives. She saw tenderness, passionate encounters and long, gentle nights.

She shivered, dealing with her pride, weighing it against a lifetime with Jake. "So," she managed in an uneven, high voice. "Are we talking contract? What are the specs? And . . . ah, Jake do you think I could care for the horses now?"

Then more firmly, with a glowing smile and her heart bursting joyously, she said, "Yes. I'll marry you."

Jake scooped her into his arms, grinning rakishly. His kiss was hard, passionate, leaving her stunned. The new secretary leapt to her feet as he swept by her desk, carrying Morganna, who snuggled against him. "I'm getting married," she said simply. "I'll be out of touch for a few days."

Seven hours later, Morganna looked up at Jake, who had just finished making love to her. His eyes were tender, filled with love, his heart slowing gradually against her breast. She smoothed back a sleek strand of hair from his rough cheek, running her thumb across his slightly swollen bottom lip. "I love this sleeping bag, dear heart."

Reluctant to leave her body, Jake rested lightly over her. Morganna stroked his back, soothing the rippling, trembling muscles. The meadow where they met was soft with summer, the night shadows sweeping down from the rugged mountains. Her new Appaloosa mare grazed with Black Jack and Pinky a distance away. The raven was stalking over her underwear, the scarlet running shorts and top were tangled and tossed on top of a nearby bush. Jake's boots and jeans lay where they had been jerked free, and his torn shirt—she'd been a bit eager—rested on the lush meadow grass.

Jake had flown the helicopter to an airfield not far from Kansas City, collecting a pilot who had deposited them in the field. Tyree and Paul, who had brought supplies and horses, immediately returned to the ranch. The beautiful mare was another bridal gift, but the most precious gift of all was Jake's fervent, "You are my wife from this day forward . . . you are my sunlight, my rainbow, my heart."

Their ceremony, the bonding of their hearts, had begun, the wedding would take place later. He insisted that traditional ceremonies were important and demanded "a white wedding gown, a church, and the entire family there."

She kissed Jake's flushed cheek, and he turned slightly, meeting her lips. The kiss was long and sweet just as their lives would be.

"Blossom," he whispered tenderly before the kiss changed, sliding into passion.

Epilogue

Two years later Jake stood in the center of the meadow, dressed in his jeans. The morning mist swirled around him. The droplets clung to his skin, his hair. A beaver moved along the creek, worrying a stripling tree that would soon topple.

Jake let the peace he had found flow through him, absorbed the joy circling his heart, lifting his soul. His wife was sleeping in their camp, weary after a long night of sharing their hearts and bodies beneath the starry sky. So it was meant to be, so it would be, he said silently to those who had loved before him, his mother and father and those beyond them.

The colors of sun and wind, earth and sky swirled, shimmering in the mist, the dawn sweeping away the haze. He breathed deeply, thinking of their daughter, Lomasi, who snuggled in the tent with her mother. In the Native American language, Lomasi meant "pretty flower," an apt description for his daughter. He remembered her birth, the tears he had shed and Morganna's indignant cry, "*We* push?

We breathe?... What do you mean, *we,* Jake? If I'm not up to tending the livestock after this, we are having an in-depth conference.''

After Lomasi's birth, Morganna had cuddled the baby, her eyes shining up at him. ''I do love you, Jake Tallman.''

When he had bent to kiss her, she'd smoothed his hair. ''You fainted, dear heart,'' she'd reminded him gently, her soft green eyes tender with love. Then he had given her the traditional family gift from a man to the mother of his child, a blossom-shaped ring of green, shimmering gemstone, and she had cried softly in his arms.

Jake traced the flight of deer crossing the meadow to water at the creek. The peace in his heart spread, lifted away the yesterdays and filled him with tomorrows.

Morganna had insisted that he show his paintings, and the rejection that Jake ultimately feared never came. He was stunned at the prices that the paintings, so near his heart, his soul, brought from patrons. Morganna worked in his studio—the old ranch house, now attached to a spacious new home—alternately adding pieces to her quilts and freewheeling Larrimore's business through her telephone, fax, and computer setups. The old cabin served as their private nest, hoarding moments away from the invasions of Larrimores, Tyree, Paul and Petey.

Petey was completely immersed in his own brand of freewheeling—housekeeping and baby tending at odd moments. Enchanted with Lomasi, Petey was a push-over for the busy, agile toddler. He had hovered worriedly through her first steps and fussed when she teethed. Despite the strain, Petey appeared younger, quite happy with the busy flow through the house. At the moment he was feverishly working on a big ''blowout'' to show off Jake's new collection and the house. The ''blowout'' was also to celebrate Tyree's high school graduation and the trade school's, Jasmine Technical's, second successful year. He had given Jake orders to keep ''Miss Blossom away for a few days.''

''Da,'' the child's sleepy voice surprised Jake and he bent to scoop Lomasi into his arms. A miniature Morganna, she cuddled against him, her sleek black hair framing her pale face and drowsy green eyes. Drawing her blanket, a satin patchwork made by her mother, around Lomasi, Jake swayed with her, filled with awe. This small bit of Morganna and himself had made their life even better. "Da, Mama...." Lomasi said against his throat. "Mama cook...."

Jake's eyes jerked to their campsite. Dressed in his flannel shirt, socks, and her moccasins, Morganna waved cheerfully over a blazing fire. A fire that he had just banked after making biscuits and coffee.

After breakfast Lomasi toddled after a butterfly, and Morganna glowered at Jake. While Jake admired the view of long, smooth legs and a tantalizing glimpse of milky breast beneath the flannel shirt, she wiggled the toes of her moccasins near the fire and sipped on her cup of herbal tea. "This camping thing isn't an exclusive male right, you know, Mr. Tallman. You have no business hoarding all the fun, sweeping out of the mist like that at a dead run. Lomasi was giggling so hard, she didn't understand the seriousness of your highhanded takeover. She's going to get the idea that every time you want to settle an argument quickly, you use that darn, mind-blowing kiss. I know I can handle this camping thing. I've got a whole new set of manuals. Back off."

"We could see just what you can handle," he offered slowly, huskily. "Though you woke up a few animals last night."

He grinned when Morganna's eyes widened and she blushed, floundering a bit and thoroughly enchanting him. Then she met his grin. "We'll see who wakes up the animals first tonight, dear heart," she challenged with a wink. Scampering to her feet, she ran after Lomasi who was trying to climb a tree after her butterfly.

Settling back to enjoy the sight of his wife and child frolicking amid the meadow's wildflowers, Jake began to design his next gift for Morganna. She hadn't told him yet, but the signs were there. Her body was preparing for another child.

The sunlight warmed him, tangled in his heart. So it would be, so it would be. The song would go on forever.

*   *   *   *   *

Take 4 bestselling love stories FREE

Plus get a FREE surprise gift!

Special Limited-time Offer

Mail to Silhouette Reader Service™

P.O. Box 609
Fort Erie, Ontario
L2A 5X3

YES! Please send me 4 free Silhouette Desire® novels and my free surprise gift. Then send me 6 brand-new novels every month, which I will receive months before they appear in bookstores. Bill me at the low price of $2.49 each plus 25¢ delivery and GST*. That's the complete price and—compared to the cover prices of $2.99 each—quite a bargain! I understand that accepting the books and gift places me under no obligation ever to buy any books. I can always return a shipment and cancel at any time. Even if I never buy another book from Silhouette, the 4 free books and the surprise gift are mine to keep forever.

326 BPA AJJ3

Name	(PLEASE PRINT)	
Address	Apt. No.	
City	Province	Postal Code

 **SILHOUETTE® Desire®**

 SOMETHING Wild

by Ann Major

Take a walk on the wild side with Ann Major's sizzling stories featuring Honey, Midnight...and Innocence!

IN SEPTEMBER, YOU EXPERIENCED...

WILD HONEY Man of the Month
A clash of wills set the stage for an electrifying romance for J. K. Cameron and Honey Wyatt.

NOW ENJOY...

WILD MIDNIGHT November 1993
Heat Up Your Winter
A bittersweet reunion turns into a once-in-a-lifetime adventure for Lacy Douglas and Johnny Midnight.

AND IN FEBRUARY 1994, LOOK FOR...

WILD INNOCENCE Man of the Month
One man's return sets off a startling chain of events for Innocence Lescuer and Raven Wyatt.

Let your wilder side take over with this exciting series—only from Silhouette Desire!

▼™ SILHOUETTE® *Desire*®

HAS THE WINTER WEATHER GOT YOU DOWN? IS THE TEMPERATURE JUST TOO COLD? THEN

COMING IN NOVEMBER ONLY FROM SILHOUETTE DESIRE

Silhouette Desire's most sensuous writers bring you six sexy stories—and six stunning heroes—guaranteed to get your temperature rising.

Look for

#817	**TWEED** by Lass Small
#818	**NOT JUST ANOTHER PERFECT WIFE** by Robin Elliott
#819	**WILD MIDNIGHT** by Ann Major
#820	**KEEGAN'S HUNT** by Dixie Browning
#821	**THE BEST REVENGE** by Barbara Boswell
#822	**DANCLER'S WOMAN** by Mary Lynn Baxter

When it comes to sinfully seductive heroes and provocative love stories...no one does it better than Silhouette Desire!

SDWH

Silhouette Books has done it again!

Opening night in October has never been as exciting! Come watch as the curtain rises and romance flourishes when the stars of tomorrow make their debuts today!

Revel in Jodi O'Donnell's STILL SWEET ON HIM—
Silhouette Romance #969
...as Callie Farrell's renovation of the family homestead leads her straight into the arms of teenage crush Drew Barnett!

Tingle with Carol Devine's BEAUTY AND THE BEASTMASTER—
Silhouette Desire #816
...as legal eagle Amanda Tarkington is carried off by wrestler Bram Masterson!

Thrill to Elyn Day's A BED OF ROSES—
Silhouette Special Edition #846
...as Dana Whitaker's body and soul are healed by sexy physical therapist Michael Gordon!

Believe when Kylie Brant's McLAIN'S LAW —
Silhouette Intimate Moments #528
...takes you into detective Connor McLain's life as he falls for psychic—and suspect—Michele Easton!

Catch the classics of tomorrow—*premiering* today—
only from V. Silhouette

SILHOUETTE.... Where Passion Lives

Don't miss these Silhouette favorites by some of our most popular authors!
And now, you can receive a discount by ordering two or more titles!

Silhouette Desire®

#05751	THE MAN WITH THE MIDNIGHT EYES BJ James	$2.89	☐
#05763	THE COWBOY Cait London	$2.89	☐
#05774	TENNESSEE WALTZ Jackie Merritt	$2.89	☐
#05779	THE RANCHER AND THE RUNAWAY BRIDE Joan Johnston	$2.89	☐

Silhouette Intimate Moments®

#07417	WOLF AND THE ANGEL Kathleen Creighton	$3.29	☐
#07480	DIAMOND WILLOW Kathleen Eagle	$3.39	☐
#07486	MEMORIES OF LAURA Marilyn Pappano	$3.39	☐
#07493	QUINN EISLEY'S WAR Patricia Gardner Evans	$3.39	☐

Silhouette Shadows®

#27003	STRANGER IN THE MIST Lee Karr	$3.50	☐
#27007	FLASHBACK Terri Herrington	$3.50	☐
#27009	BREAK THE NIGHT Anne Stuart	$3.50	☐
#27012	DARK ENCHANTMENT Jane Toombs	$3.50	☐

Silhouette Special Edition®

#09754	THERE AND NOW Linda Lael Miller	$3.39	☐
#09770	FATHER: UNKNOWN Andrea Edwards	$3.39	☐
#09791	THE CAT THAT LIVED ON PARK AVENUE Tracy Sinclair	$3.39	☐
#09811	HE'S THE RICH BOY Lisa Jackson	$3.39	☐

Silhouette Romance®

#08893	LETTERS FROM HOME Toni Collins	$2.69	☐
#08915	NEW YEAR'S BABY Stella Bagwell	$2.69	☐
#08927	THE PURSUIT OF HAPPINESS Anne Peters	$2.69	☐
#08952	INSTANT FATHER Lucy Gordon	$2.75	☐

	AMOUNT	$ _____
DEDUCT:	10% DISCOUNT FOR 2+ BOOKS	$ _____
	POSTAGE & HANDLING	$ _____
	($1.00 for one book, 50¢ for each additional)	
	APPLICABLE TAXES*	$ _____
	TOTAL PAYABLE	$ _____
	(check or money order—please do not send cash)	

To order, complete this form and send it, along with a check or money order for the total above, payable to Silhouette Books, to: *In the U.S.*: 3010 Walden Avenue, P.O. Box 9077, Buffalo, NY 14269-9077; *In Canada*: P.O. Box 636, Fort Erie, Ontario, L2A 5X3.

Name: _____

Address: _____ City: _____

State/Prov.: _____ Zip/Postal Code: _____

*New York residents remit applicable sales taxes.
Canadian residents remit applicable GST and provincial taxes.

SBACK-OD

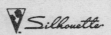